Jessica's King

King Brother Investigation Series

Clarice Jayne

To Jackie

I hope you enjoy

Clarice Jayne

Contents

Dedication

A big thank you goes out to, Stephanie, Debs, Beatrix and Carol for all your help and support. For sparing your time reading through my book and helping me along the way. Without which, Jessica's King would never have got published.

Thank you to you all.

Chapter One

Mason

Monday mornings, how I hated them! Always the same thing...we had the morning meeting with the team discussing everything that had happened over the weekend. I was in the conference room with the team sitting around me, not really paying attention to anything that was being said. It was just a typical start of the week.

I listened to them drone on as usual about how this client's wife had been with her lover all weekend in bed, or how the husband had been shopping for expensive gifts that she would never receive. It always brought me back to the same thought. Cassandra!

It had been nearly three years since I found out the truth. I had not long left the SAS and had started up the King Brothers Investigation business with Brandon, knowing that my brother Jayden and his best friends Tyler and Nathan would join us in a couple of years, once they left the Army. Everything was perfect. I was finally hoping to settle down, get married, and raise a family with her. That was, until the day Brandon came to see me.

He had been my best friend for years. We had struck up our friendship from the first day we enlisted. Wherever I went he was with me, as if he was my own shadow. Together we travelled the world serving our Queen and Country, seeing sights that would cause most men to lose the plot. We spent so much time with each other that we were more like brothers than friends.

I can still remember that day like it was yesterday. He walked into my flat with the pictures in his hand and told me the unfortunate truth. I had always suspected that she was being unfaithful to me while I was on deployment, but I didn't want to believe it. I couldn't believe it. However, there it was in full colour, Cassandra in the arms of another man!

It had been one of the first jobs I had sent Brandon on. A wife suspected that her husband was having an affair. Brandon had spent the whole week tailing the husband. He had done all the usual things, spent time working in his office, a round of golf with his business partners, nothing out of the ordinary for a top executive.

That was, until Friday night. Instead of going home to his wife like he had done for the rest of the week, he paid a visit to a West End hotel. That was when Brandon saw her walking into the hotel and straight up to the cheating husband. Little did we know when we took the job that not only was he having an affair, but it was with my fiancé!

I had known something was wrong as soon as Brandon walked in, the look on his face said it all. The only thing he could say when he placed the photos on the coffee table was "I'm sorry". I sat there looking at them for what seemed like hours. How he had gotten the pictures in the hotel room I would never know, but he had, and that was all that mattered to me.

Cassandra was there, lying on the bed with another man, my beautiful fiancé in the throes of passion. There was no mistaking it was her; I would recognise the look on that face anywhere, because it was the same look she had always given me.

I sat in the conference room lost in my thoughts, when I was suddenly pulled back to the present.

"Hello, Earth to Mason King!" Jayden suddenly said.

"Yeah, we should definitely do that," I replied, not even knowing what I was agreeing we should do.

"Have you actually been listening to any of the conversation this morning, or are you completely lost in your own thoughts again? It's the same every Monday morning, I'm not even sure why you bother holding these meetings, bro."

I looked over at him and to the rest of the guys who were all now staring at me as though waiting for me to crack.

"Sorry, I didn't get much sleep last night, must just still be tired. You guys know exactly what needs to be done, so just let me know what you have decided. I have some paperwork to do, so you can find me in my office. I'll catch you all later."

I stood up from the conference table and headed down the corridor to my office and sat down at my desk. Jayden was right. It was the same every Monday morning. It had been three years, but I still couldn't get those images out of my head. I was always asking myself the same questions, what had I done wrong? Why did she cheat on me? How could I have made things better?

I knew those were probably the exact same questions our clients asked themselves when we showed them proof of their partner's infidelity. Unfortunately, I couldn't answer them for our clients, and I had never been able to answer them for myself.

There was a knock on my office door.

"Come in, door's open," I said, looking up to see Brandon walking through the door. I laughed to myself; he never waited for me to tell him to come in unless he knew I was with a new client.

"Hey, Brandon, what's up?" I asked as he took a chair in front of my desk.

"Shouldn't I be asking you that question?" He sat down and continued. "Mace, it's been three years already. You have got to let her go, it's still eating you up inside, and I can't stand to see you like this every Monday morning!"

"Brandon, how can I forget? I'm reminded every single day of what happened to me. We are in the business of investigating cheating husbands, wives, and partners for fuck's sake! How can I forget what she did to me?"

"I know it's hard, Mace, but you have to snap out of it! I worry every damn weekend that I'm going to show up and find you in a drunken coma in your place again. I can't see you like that again, bro. It nearly killed Jayden and me!"

Now that was a weekend to forget. Well, for the most part I couldn't recollect anything about it, and that was probably a good thing. It was the weekend after I had found out the truth. I had been avoiding Cassandra all week, making excuses for why I couldn't see her. I knew she suspected something. She had become very clingy, calling and texting me every hour worried about where I was and what I was doing. It was almost as though she suspected me of being in the wrong.

I had arranged to meet her at her flat in Chelsea, the one I had originally gotten for her and was paying for. That stopped that very night. There was no way I was paying the rent of a woman that was never going to be mine.

Cassandra opened the door to her flat and embraced me as she would usually do. However, everything had changed in those five days we had been apart. There was no spark. The feelings I always had whenever she touched me had gone forever. This time, all I felt was hurt, pain, and coldness in her touch.

She had treated me as her meal ticket for all those years, and got exactly what she wanted from me. An expensive flat, clothes, jewellery, and I had done it willingly because I loved her and wanted to spend the rest of my life with her. I wondered how many different men she had slept with over the years.

Without a word, I walked past her and into the living room. I could tell from the way she was looking at me that she was confused and worried. I made her sit down on the settee and before she could say a word, I dropped copies of the photographs onto the coffee table. The look of shock, anger, and complete disgust on her face gave me all the answers I needed. Then I turned to her.

"I can see from those that you've made your decision, and you no longer want to be with me. The flat is in your name, exactly the way you wanted it. You can pay for it, and don't think of using any of the credit cards as they have all been stopped!"

I didn't give her any time to explain. I just turned my back and walked out of the door to the sounds of her hysterical screams. I went back to my flat and turned off my phone after receiving countless texts and calls from her trying to explain her way out of everything. I opened the cupboard and got out a bottle of scotch and a glass.

After that, nothing! The rest of the weekend was blank! Brandon and Jayden found me Monday morning unconscious in my living room on the settee. They had been trying to contact me after Cassandra had called them in hysterics on Saturday. Knowing me to be a level-headed, sensible guy, they hadn't worried, deciding to give me some space until I didn't show up at the office on Monday.

According to the guys there were two bottles of scotch lying empty in the room and I had been lucky not to die of alcohol poisoning.

I looked up at Brandon as my focus came back to the present. I could see the worry and concern in his eyes. I knew Jayden was worried too, which was probably why he had sent Brandon in here. Jayden knew Brandon could get through to me when he couldn't.

"I'm fine, Brandon. And you can let my brother know that as well. I know he sent you in here."

"We both worry about you, Mace. Fuck, even Tyler and Nathan worry about you. You know they look up to you like a big brother! We just want the old Mason back, the carefree guy we could go down to the pub with and have a few beers. Even when we all have a weekend off, you find some excuse not to come."

"OK, I get it! Next time you all go out I will come too, but no strip clubs. Remember the last time?"

"Hell yeah, I do! Sounds like a good idea to me."

Brandon started to walk out the door. "Brandon! I said no strip clubs!" I called after him as he turned down the corridor to his office.

"Yeah, yeah, whatever!" He called back.

I chuckled to myself and started to shake my head. Yep, that was a disaster in the making, I could tell already.

I opened up my schedule for the day. For a Monday it was quite empty for a change. The only thing scheduled was a meeting this afternoon at our London office with a possible new client. I hated going there and tried to avoid it at all costs, however it was where most of our clients were based.

The core of our clientele were professionals working in town; therefore, it made sense to have a base in the city. However, the building held far too many bad memories for me. Everywhere I turned there were reminders of her. She had helped me choose the offices and decorate them to make them welcoming to both male and female clients.

That was why I had to relocate here in Kings View. Yes, I know it is kind of corny moving to a town with the same name as your surname, but that was exactly why I chose it. It was just a small town, almost a village, but I loved it here. It had everything I needed, a coffee shop, restaurant, pub, a small high street, and a supermarket.

I bought a cottage just outside the town overlooking the beautifully green and hilly countryside of the South Downs National Park. The rest of the guys hated it, too old and 'fuddy-duddy' they said, but for me it was perfect. It was what most people would describe as quaint, but it was far from small.

It was a three-bedroom cottage on an acre of land. I had a range cooker in the kitchen, keeping it lovely and cosy in the winter. In the sitting room I had a log burner which was used every winter, not to keep warm, but just because there was something comforting about having a real fire in the house. I was also lucky enough to have a large conservatory on the back overlooking the downs. Luckily, the cottage was not a listed building, so additions like this were allowed.

I could relax there and go on long walks in the countryside with Monty, my Sprocker Spaniel, my dependable companion. I had always wanted a dog, but living in a flat in the centre of London didn't lend itself to animals. Living out in the country allowed me to finally fulfil this one wish, and his love and loyalty was all I needed now.

We were only just over an hour away from London, which was a benefit both for work and fun, not that I had much of that recently. Perhaps the guys were right, perhaps I did need to get out more? I didn't want to be in a relationship, hell, I had enough of love and romance to last me a lifetime, but that shouldn't stop me from having a good time.

I went over the details I had for the meeting this afternoon, definitely more interesting than our usual jobs. The owner of a web design company was positive he was losing clients to one of his members of staff working privately and undercutting them.

I knew this was going to be a long-term job, seeing as these kinds of investigations had to be squeaky clean so criminal prosecutions could take place if required. However, they paid really well, and good results lead to recommendations and more work in the long run, so it was important to get it right.

I knew it would be a job that would be right up Tyler's street; he was the techie geek of the company and would enjoy the challenge. If we got the job, then this was one he would definitely take the lead on.

I read through all the information that the potential client had sent through to me, making notes and writing questions that I wanted to ask, so I was well prepared for the meeting.

After what felt like forever, I looked over at the clock on the wall. 11:45, time to go and grab something to eat before I headed into the city. And I knew exactly where to go, Jessica's Coffee House. For lunch, it was really the only place to go unless you wanted a pre-packed sandwich from the local supermarket.

Brushing all of my memories off my shoulders, I got up from my desk and headed out of my office. I made sure to make a passing comment to Jayden, saying I was grabbing some lunch, then I walked through the main office doors and out onto the street to focus on my day ahead

Chapter Two

Jessica

The blaring sound of my alarm abruptly woke me from a deep sleep. 4:30 a.m. already. Still drowsy from one of the best night's sleep I'd had in ages, I rolled over, hit the off button, then I stretched out the final sleepiness from my body. Another Monday morning...at least it was the least busy day of the week, especially in Kings View in the autumn.

Spring and summer were always busy with holiday makers passing through the town to stay down on the coast or to visit the beautiful countryside of the South Downs. However, once autumn arrived the passing trade started to fade, and I was left with my loyal customers, the people of Kings View. I knew I wasn't ever going to make a fortune, but I got by just fine. To me, the love I felt for my little shop and everyone in the town was enough.

As the boiler lit up, signalling that the heating had just kicked in, I realized that I really needed to change the timer on the system. By the time the flat was actually getting warm I was walking out the door. The problem was, I was useless at that kind of thing, and every time I did try to change it, I just made matters worse. I made a mental note to have a word with Chris, my neighbour; he was always good at that kind of thing and willing to help.

Without thinking, I threw back the covers on my bed and immediately regretted it. The cold air in my bedroom sent shivers through my entire body. Yes, I really needed to get that damn timer changed. Also, a hot shower was definitely required to kick me into gear this morning. I got out of bed, shivers still running through me, and walked across the corridor to my bathroom. Once I walked in, I immediately turned the shower on, setting it on as hot as I thought I could bear, then I looked in the mirror.

I never considered myself to be beautiful or pretty, most women didn't, but I never thought I was plain either. I was a normal woman with curves in the right places, who would possibly be attractive to the right man, just not to anyone in Kings View. Even if there was someone to impress in town, I wouldn't be doing that today with the bed head I was currently sporting. Chuckling at the thought, I picked the tooth brush up, added some toothpaste and quickly set about brushing my teeth.

Once done, I pulled off my pjs and stood under the welcoming heat of the shower. How I wished I could stay here all day. Unfortunately, I had plenty to do at the coffee shop. With that in mind, I quickly washed my hair and body, switched off the shower, and wrapped myself in the biggest towel I owned. There was no time to dry my hair, so it would have to be towel dried and wrapped up into a bun for the day. I'd deal with the mess that would cause when I got home tonight.

After pulling on my favourite skinny jeans, t shirt and jumper, I folded the pjs and put them on top of my pillow, ready for tonight. Walking out of my bedroom and to the front door, I headed out of the flat and down to my coffee shop below to start my daily routine.

One benefit of where I lived was the short journey to work each day. Conveniently, my flat was right above the shop. It was placed on the end of a row of shops in the high street of Kings View, which included the bank, pharmacy, and newsagents, and above was four flats. It was like living in a small community. My flat was on the end of the terrace of shops. Next to me was Christopher Carter, then Mr. and Mrs. Duncan who owned and ran the Newsagents, and at the end was Madeleine Lewis, or Maddie for short.

Maddie was a student and would spend a lot of time in the coffee shop studying. She loved it there, watching the world go by while she was working through her online course. I didn't complain, as she would often help out around the coffee shop whenever it got busy. I had offered to pay her countless times, but Maddie would never accept any money, but would always have free coffee whenever she was in.

I walked down the stairs to the street below and opened the door at the back of my shop. Then I turned on the lights and proceeded to get everything ready for the morning. As usual, I had made all the pastries, rolls, and bread the night before so they were all ready to put in the oven to bake. Turning on the ovens, I placed all the trays in to start cooking while I went to the front of the shop to start making myself a coffee.

As I stood waiting for the coffee to come through the machine, I thought about how nice it would be to have a latte, but at this time in the morning, filter coffee did the job just as well. Then I remembered the day I had first opened the shop. It was six years ago now. My Mum and Dad had still lived in the town then and were so proud that I was starting up my own business. I hadn't wanted much out of life, because quite frankly I wasn't academically minded, but I did love to cook and bake.

Working in a restaurant had never interested me. All those long hours being bossed around by a chef just didn't suit me. I wanted to own my own place. So when Mr. and Mrs. Baker retired as the owners of the then called Cafe Shack, I jumped at the chance to open it. The local Bank Manager helped me with the loan to purchase the business and that was it, Jessica's Coffee House was born.

I could still recall the look on my parents' faces the day I opened; their eyes were so full of pride. We were overwhelmed by the number of people from the town that came in to wish me well, including the Bakers. Everything was perfect, business was booming, and although I was working from dawn to dusk, the money coming in was good, and I actually enjoyed my day.

That was until that fateful day five years ago when my Mum died. It had been so sudden and unexpected. She had had a short illness and her health had gone down rapidly. It was only in her final days that the doctors established she had breast cancer and it was too late. We were devastated! My dad changed overnight from the fun loving person I adored to a shell of his former self. After a few months he decided that he couldn't live in Kings View anymore and sold the house and moved down to Eastbourne to be near his sister and her family.

There was absolutely no way I could move. I had to stay and continue to run the business, so I was now here in Kings View alone. Over the years Dad had become more like his own self and had started seeing a lovely lady called Edith. She made him happy, and that was all that mattered to me. I knew it would never be the same as having my own mum back, but I had grown to love her and enjoyed when they came up from the coast to visit.

Lost in thought, I grabbed the coffee pot that had finished brewing and poured myself a mug. I had just put the jug down when there was a knock at the shop door. Confused, I looked up at the clock, reading 5:30 a.m. It wasn't unusual for someone to come to the shop before I opened at 7:00, but this was a lot earlier than usual.

Curious, I walked from behind the counter and over to the door to look and see who it was. A sigh of relief fell from my lips when I realised it was just my next door neighbour Chris. I gestured to him that I'd just be a minute, then I headed out back to get the keys to unlock. Walking back to the front of the shop, I proceeded to unlock the door before opening it and greeting Chris with a smile.

"God morning, Chris. You're early today," I said cheerfully.

"Morning, Jess. Yeah, sorry about that. I have an early start today and was hoping to grab a coffee and a Danish before I left."

"I only have what's left over from yesterday as today's are still in the oven. They should still be good, though. Hazelnut Latte?"

"You know me too well, Jess, and yesterday's Danish will be fine, thank you so much."

"I have some rolls left if you would like me to make you something for your lunch," I informed him.

"No, it's fine. I will grab something on the job."

"It's not a problem at all."

"No, really, it's fine," he replied smiling at me, as I turned to the coffee machine and started to make his Latte. Once done, I bagged up a couple of his favourite Danish and handed them over to him.

"It's on the house," I said as he took the bag and coffee mug.

"You won't make any money if you do things like that all the time. I insist that I pay." He proceeded to take his wallet out of his pocket.

"No, it's fine, I actually wanted to ask you for a favour, so call it pay back for that."

"And what's the favour?" He asked, a smirk falling across his face.

"Nothing like that, for fuck's sake! Get your mind out of the gutter." I laughed. "Could you come and have a look at the timer on my heating and hot water. You know how rubbish I am with that type of thing."

He laughed, "How many times is this now? Of course, I will pop round when you finish tonight. 7 o'clock OK for you?"

"That would be brilliant, and thank you."

"Anytime. babe. Thanks for the coffee. I'll see you later, and don't forget to lock up after I leave."

"I won't, see you later." I replied and followed him as he turned and walked out of the shop.

I locked the door and paused for a second thinking about what Chris had just said. He had called me babe. He had never done that before. I insisted from the beginning that he call me Jess, since I did not like to be called Jessica all the time, but he had never called me babe.

He was a really nice guy, not really my type, but I could see how some women would find him attractive. He was always polite and was a true gentleman. Chris just didn't do it for me, though I couldn't explain why, there was just something about him.

I mentally shrugged my shoulders. He probably just said it as a term of endearment to say thanks for the coffee. Nodding to myself, I went back into the kitchen and removed the first batch of pastries from the oven and swapped for the next batch to be cooked. Two batches were more than enough for a Monday, since usually by the end of the day I was giving them away to anyone that was having a coffee just so I didn't throw them away.

I placed the pastries on the trays ready to go out into the display cabinets once they had cooled thoroughly. Before I knew it all my rolls, bread, and pastries were cooked, and it was 6.30 and nearly time to open. I had just put out the last tray of pastries into the cabinet when a knock at the door signalled my first customer of the day.

I knew exactly who it would be and started the coffee machine for the two lattes that they would order. I walked over to the shop door, unlocked and opened it.

"Good morning, Mr. Duncan. How are you and your lovely wife this morning?"

"Good morning, Jess. We are both very well, and how many times have I told you, call me George," he replied with a chuckle.

"Too many to remember, but I was always brought up to respect my elders, and that includes calling anyone around the same age as my parents as Mr. and Mrs., and I would not want to let them down," I replied with a smile.

"I don't know, Jess. What am I going to do with you? How are your Dad and Edith? It seems like forever since they were last up here."

"They are both well, should be here in a couple of weeks, actually. I will let them know you asked after them." I turned back to the coffee machine to finish the two lattes for Mr. Duncan.

"You do realise that you can make a coffee in your own shop, don't you Mr. Duncan?" I pointed out, turning and placing them on the counter.

"Yes, I know my dear, but then I wouldn't get to speak to my favourite coffee shop owner every morning. Plus, you make the best lattes and pastries in town, so why wouldn't I come here every morning."

"Mr. Duncan, I do believe that I'm the only one that serves coffee and pastries throughout the day, so I'm not sure that's a valid reason," I laughed, while placing two pain au chocolat into a bag and handing them over.

"There you go, Mr. Duncan. I hope you and Mrs. Duncan enjoy them."

"I'm sure we will, we always do, Jess sweetie. Can we have our usual order for lunch, please, and I will pick it up around 1 p.m. if that is OK?" He handed over the exact same amount of money as usual.

"Not a problem. I will have it all ready for you then. Can you ask Mrs. Duncan to pop round when she has a minute? I have an idea I would like to run past her for some new lunch ideas, if that's OK."

"Will do. Have a good day, Jess, and I will see you later for my lunch."

"Will do, thank you, and you too," I called after him and continued to get everything ready for the morning.

There was nothing special about that morning. My regular customers came and went. In between serving customers, I got my orders ready for pick up during the day. I even got to sit down and spend some time with Maddie, who was in her usual spot for the day.

We had been chatting about this and that for a while when the bell on the shop door rang indicating a customer had walked in. I looked up to see a tall, dark, and well-dressed man walk in. I was sure I'd seen him around town occasionally, but I never knew who he really was.

"Good afternoon, how can I help you?" I asked as I made my way behind the counter.

"Afternoon, could I please have a chicken salad baguette and a latte to take away please?"

"Would you prefer a white or granary baguette?"

"A granary baguette would be great, thank you."

"Take a seat, and I will bring it over to you when it's ready."

"Thank you," He simply said, then took a seat at one of the empty tables in the shop.

Not wasting any time, I quickly got to work making the baguette, wrapping it in paper and cutting it in half before putting it in a bag. I then made the latte and took it over to where the dashing gentleman sat. Smiling politely, I said, "There you go. All ready for you. I hope you enjoy it."

"I'm sure I will, thank you." He gazed at my eyes for just a moment, causing butterflies to flutter in my stomach then walked over to the counter, and handed over the payment. Then he left the shop.

"Who was that?" Maddie turned to me and asked.

I responded a little breathy, "I'm not sure. I think he works at that Private Investigator's up the road."

"Well, he is a little old for me, but absolutely perfect for you, Jess. You really should find out who he is." Maddie wiggled her eyebrows suggestively.

"Don't be silly. He wouldn't be interested in me, and even if he was, not only am I not looking for anyone, but I really don't have the time." I shrugged.

"I was just saying." Maddie laughed and continued to get on with her work.

I stood there for a moment taking in what Maddie said. Who was I kidding? The man was gorgeous, he'd never be interested in me. I sighed to myself and went about cleaning everywhere to save time later in the day.

Chapter Three

Mason

Sitting in the train carriage on the way back from the office, I went through all the notes I had made at the meeting with Mr. Jarvis regarding the issues he was facing. It did appear that there was some form of moonlighting going on by an employee. The issue was, how did we prove it?

Mr. Jarvis had lost clients over the past year, many of which were about to sign the contract with his company. As a Web Design business, he knew that competition was great, and many potential customers decided to go elsewhere. However, losing clients so close to the signatures just didn't make sense.

He would look at their websites a few months later and see that they had been re-designed by a mystery person or company. The reason it was a mystery was because there was no name shown on the pages. Most companies when designing a website would have a link to their design company, as it was always part of the contract to promote their business. The new pages looked as though they had been designed in-house, which he couldn't comprehend as they had previously been looking to buy services.

Contemplating everything that had been discussed, I decided that the best course of action was to get someone on the inside. If I sent Tyler in there, he would be able to get to know the staff and find the most logical culprit. Mr. Jarvis had his suspicions, but could not be 100 percent sure, as they were careful.

Tyler was good at what he did. As our techie geek he had designed the company website. Anything we needed regarding new technology, he either had or could get hold of quickly. His skills would be perfect to pose as a new employee for Mr. Jarvis and shouldn't raise any suspicions, especially as the company had just lost a web designer to another firm and was currently recruiting.

Looking out the window, I could see the final streets and buildings of the city going past and the rural countryside start to appear. The tension I had been feeling about being back in London started to fade and I almost felt at peace. I briefly had a random flash of the woman in the coffee shop cross my memory. Not sure why, I brushed it off. Turning my attention back to my laptop, I started to look through my emails for the day.

Nothing out of the ordinary, just the normal updates from the guys about what they had found out regarding their cases. We also had a few freelance investigators working for us sending in their reports from the weekend. They would come in handy if we wanted to expand the business like I was considering. They could either come on board as full time staff or would have to renegotiate their terms as it was currently costing us a fortune.

Shutting down my laptop, I packed everything away in my bag and settled down for the last half hour of my journey. It was always more relaxing to take the train. Although I didn't mind driving, it was always a pain trying to get in and out of London, and what should be an hour long journey, often took me around two to three hours.

Picking up my phone, I started to scroll through my social media pages. As usual they were filled with rubbish that really didn't interest me. Why I bothered to join half of them I really didn't know. It was only because my brother and Tyler said I needed a presence on them for the good of the business. To be fair, they really didn't interest me, it was more their thing being that bit younger than me.

My phone started to ring just as I was about to put it away in my bag. Looking down at the caller ID, I saw it was Jayden.

"Hey bro, what's up?" I asked.

"Are you on your way back now?"

"Yeah, just coming up to Kings View station now. I was going to head straight home. Do you need me to come by the office before I do?"

"If you don't mind, I just need to run a couple of things past you so one of the investigators can go out tonight."

"OK, I will be there in about ten minutes, make sure you have a coffee waiting for me." I said chuckling, knowing the response I was about to get.

"Am I your PA now? You can get your own coffee on the way in, Mace." He had just confirmed what I knew had been coming.

"I could, but it wouldn't be as nice. Anyway, I am just pulling into the station now, so now you only have five minutes." I disconnected the call before he could argue any more.

Pissing my brother off gave me great satisfaction. Don't get me wrong, he gave as good as he got, but being the eldest, I always got my way. Well, except in the case of my parents, Jayden was always the blue-eyed boy who could do nothing wrong in their eyes. Laughing silently to myself, I picked up my things and made my way to the carriage doors to get off at my stop.

Exiting the station, I took the short five-minute walk up to our offices. They weren't as swanky as the main office in London, but that wasn't what I wanted. This was my base every day, so I wanted it to be comfortable. The London office was just for show.

The rest of the guys tended to spend most of their time up there. They all lived closer to the city, so for them it made more sense, only coming here every Monday morning, and if they needed to discuss anything with me they felt they couldn't over the phone.

Walking through the front door to the office, I found Jayden stood there with a latte in his hand. A smirk on my face, I walked over to him and took the drink from him.

"Thanks, bro. I knew you wouldn't let me down." I smiled at him.

"Yeah, well, you know I can't stand it when you're grumpy, and you certainly get grumpy without caffeine," He retorted.

"You just keep thinking that, bro. I know it's because you love me, really. Anyway, what did we need to discuss?" I said, walking down to my office with Jayden in tow.

"Martin has been given some info regarding the Gardiner case and isn't sure where to go with it."

"OK, fill me in."

"Well, I think we've already established that the wife is up to something, but until this afternoon, we weren't sure what it was. Martin had a telephone call today from one of his contacts. It's rumoured that Mr. Gardiner's business is about to get a very lucrative contract from the local council," he explained.

"OK, so what has this got to do with Mrs. Gardiner having an affair?" I asked.

"Martin's contact has reason to believe that the only reason Mr. Gardiner's firm got the job was down to Mrs. Gardiner's extra marital activities."

"What do you mean, thanks to her extra marital activities?" I asked.

"Well, rumour has it, she has been sleeping with the project manager for the council that awards the contracts. Mrs. Gardiner thought that if her husband got the contract, he would be too busy to notice her infidelity."

"Well fuck, that changes matters. This could not only cost the Gardiner's their marriage, but Mr. Gardiner his business, if this kind of info escapes to the competitors."

"I know, what the fuck are we going to do?"

"Ask Martin to get confirmation on this info and then I think we need to have a chat with Mrs. Gardiner. If she doesn't listen or won't come clean to her husband, then I suppose we will have to go back to Mr. Gardiner." I started rubbing my temple.

"OK, I will get back to Martin and get him to confirm everything."

"Was there anything else you needed to discuss?" I asked.

"Nope, that's all, bro. Brandon and I are going to be working in London tomorrow, but Tyler will be here," he said.

"That's good, because I need to discuss our next job with him. He is going to have to work for the client as an employee. I suspect it is the only way we can establish exactly what is going on."

Finishing my latte, I stood up and walked around my desk.

"Anything else we need to go through before I leave, Jayden?"

"Nope, we're all good here. Everything is set for the rest of the week."

"OK, I will see you at some point then, bro." I walked over to him and gave him a hug.

"Are you going to Mum and Dad's this weekend for dinner, or are you bailing out again for a night on the town?" I asked.

"Nah, the guys are working this weekend, so I'll be there. You want me to pick you up?" he asked.

"No, I'll meet you there. I might be a bit late depending on how things go setting up the Jarvis job. I'll let Mum know, though. At least then I won't be in the doghouse."

"I hear that, bro. Talking of doghouse, are you bringing Monty with you?"

"Might do, I will see what kind of mood he's in. See you later, Jayden."

"OK, Mace."

With that I walked out of the office to make my way home for the evening.

The drive back to my place was only fifteen minutes long. In some respects it was a shame, as the countryside around the town was beautiful and I would love it to be longer. The summer was fantastic as I could either get my convertible or motorbike out, but the autumn and winter always required the 4x4. At least when I was driving that I knew I could get myself, or anyone else for that matter, out of trouble if required.

Pulling into my drive, I headed down the long dirt road to my cottage. It couldn't be seen from the main road as it was surrounded by trees, which was another reason for choosing it. Parking up outside my place, I got out of my car and could already hear an excited Monty at the front door. He always seemed to know when I was parking up and would stand barking at the door.

Opening the door, I braced myself for two paws to bound into me as usual. Unsurprisingly, I wasn't disappointed. Monty came bounding out of the door and immediately jumped towards me demanding attention. It was always a good feeling coming home to this, knowing that at least he was happy to see me. In that moment every evening was all the love and loyalty I needed.

"Come on then, boy, let's get you fed and then I can get changed and we can go for a walk," I said to him, not knowing if he really understood, but he got down and trotted right to his bowl ready to be fed.

After feeding him and making sure his water was topped up, I headed up to my bedroom and changed into jeans and a jumper ready to take him out for a walk. Monty loved to go out into the fields, especially in the autumn as he got to chase leaves around every time the wind picked them up. He would spend hours out there if I let him.

Walking back downstairs, Monty was already waiting at the front door ready to go out. Picking up his lead, I pulled on my coat and opened the front door allowing Monty to bound out and on his way. Monty hardly ever went out wearing his lead, even though he was a spaniel. I had never had any problems with his recall, and the only time I tended to use the lead was when we were around livestock.

Walking away from the house and down toward the downs on a cool autumnal afternoon was one of my favourite pastimes. Who wouldn't enjoy this? Well, I suppose it wasn't for my brother or his friends, but Brandon often joined me when he wanted to talk or clear his head.

We walked through the fields, Monty running off and then back again for a while, allowing me to just unwind from the day. This was what I needed, this was the reason I had moved out here, for the peace and quiet. Calling Monty back over to me, we headed back home. All I wanted now was a good meal and a glass of wine set in front of my log burner just to finish the day off.

Chapter Four

Jessica

"**A**nything else for you?" I asked the final customer of the day, passing over the boxes to her.

"No, that will be all, thank you. Sorry to come in so late, but I completely forgot I was meant to be bringing cakes with me tonight to my book club," the young lady replied.

"It's not a problem, to my benefit, actually. These would've all been thrown away if you hadn't come in. Hope your group enjoys them," I replied.

"Thank you, I'm sure they will, and I will definitely recommend you to them all." She smiled as she turned to go.

"Thank you so much. Have a lovely evening".

Following the young lady to the shop door, I opened it allowing her to leave, then shut and locked it. Looking up at the clock I noticed it was just after 6:00 p.m. Time to get myself into gear as Chris would be round in just under an hour.

Just as I was about to walk back to the counter, I noticed a black truck parked across the road. Funny, I don't remember anyone in town owning a vehicle like that, and it's not the tourist season. No sooner had I noticed it, it suddenly pulled away and drove off towards the other end of town. Shrugging it off as my own paranoia, I walked back to the counter.

After finishing up cleaning the counter, I turned off all the lights in the front of the shop. Walking into the back, I checked what I had left to do for the evening. Maddie had kept an eye on the shop for me this afternoon, allowing me to get ready for tomorrow. It hadn't been overly busy all day, so that gave me a chance to get some extra pastries made so I could put them into the freezer to save time later in the week.

After speaking with Mrs. Duncan this afternoon when she popped in, I had also made some Chicken and Vegetable soup. With Kings View being quite a small town there weren't many places to go for lunch. For a while now I had been toying with the idea of serving a daily special soup. Customers could either have it with a roll or a sandwich if they preferred. I wanted to discuss the idea with Mrs. Duncan as she had always helped me out with suggestions over the years. Thinking it was a fantastic idea, Mrs. Duncan had already ordered two bowls for tomorrow to go with her normal sandwich order.

Placing the pastries on trays, I put them to one side ready to cook in the morning. My thoughts wandered back to lunchtime today. For some reason I couldn't get the chicken salad baguette man out of my mind, and yes, that is what Maddie and I had now nicknamed him. He was gorgeous, tall, dark, impeccably dressed, and I just couldn't forget him.

Everything about him screamed that he was an Alpha male, but that was the problem. Guys like him would always go for the model type, and no matter what Maddie said, I was just the girl next door. There wasn't a chance he would go out with me; hell, I don't think he would even give me a second look. It would just have to stay a fantasy in my mind, one that I suspected would not allow me to sleep, but make me feel damn good.

Opening the fridge, I pulled out the small container of soup I was going to have for dinner tonight along with a couple of rolls I had left over from today. There was enough soup for two, so I thought it would be the neighbourly thing to offer some to Chris as he was so kind to help me out. Switching off the lights to the shop, I went out the back door locking it up behind me and climbed the stairs to my flat.

It was exactly 6:45 when I walked in, so I had a little under fifteen minutes to get myself sorted, and that was if Chris wasn't early. Entering my bedroom, I sensed something was wrong. Looking around, nothing seemed to be amiss, so I just put it down to my mind, still fantasizing about lunch guy.

Remembering I had to deal with the mess that was my hair, I pulled it from the bun I had created this morning. With partly wet and dry hair, I decided it was best to just go with the flow and allow it to dry naturally, so I just gave it a quick brush through and changed into a pair of jogging bottoms and a fresh top.

Going into the kitchen, I took out the soup and started to warm the rolls in the oven. With perfect timing, the doorbell rang just as I was closing the oven door. Walking over to the door, I first checked through the spy hole to make sure it was Chris before opening the door.

"Hi, Chris, thanks for coming around to help me out," I said as I gestured for him to come in.

"You know I'll always help you out, Jess. It's never a problem," He replied.

"I've got some chicken and vegetable soup and rolls warming up. Would you like to join me for dinner, by way of a thank you?" I asked.

"I thought the coffee and pastries were a thank you this morning? However, I'm not going to turn down a good home cooked meal. Thank you, I'd love to join you. I'm just going to sort out the timer on your boiler first. It should only take a few minutes."

Following Chris into the kitchen, I checked on the soup and rolls while he changed the timer on the boiler. With the soup warmed through, I took two bowls out of the cupboard and filled them full of soup, placing the rolls from the oven onto a plate and putting it all on the small table in my kitchen.

"All finished, heating will come on at 4.00 a.m., so it should be all nice and toasty when you get up."

"Thanks, Chris. Dinner is ready, so sit yourself down."

"That smells amazing, Jess. When did you have time to make this?" he asked, taking his seat at the table.

"Oh, it's nothing really, I just threw it together this afternoon. I've been thinking about serving soup in the shop for a while. After chatting with Mrs. Duncan today I decided to go for it. This was the result."

"Well damn, I think I will be getting lunch at your place more often when I am home. This tastes absolutely wonderful," he said smiling to me.

"I'm sure it's not that good, but thank you all the same. Would you like something to drink? I can do tea, coffee, water, a glass of wine?" I asked.

"Water will be just fine, thanks. I have to get up early again tomorrow. So, you can take that as your 5:30 early morning call warning, if that's OK?"

Standing to get Chris a glass of water from the fridge, I turned and replied, "I will have a hazelnut latte and pastry ready waiting for you."

We both sat in silence for a while eating our soup, which I must admit, was rather good, even though I did say so myself. Having finished my soup, I stood up from the table and placed my bowl in the sink to wash up. Turning to ask Chris if he would like a coffee, I was taken aback to find him right behind me. A slight gasp passed my lips as I felt my heart skip a beat, and unfortunately not in a good way.

"Sorry, didn't mean to make you jump." Chris said, taking a step back away from me.

"Don't worry, it's OK. Guess I'm just not used to having someone else in the flat," I replied, my breathing finally starting to slow down. "Would you like a coffee?" I asked.

"That would be great." Chris replied.

"OK, well go take a seat in the living room and I'll bring it through," I said, setting the coffee machine running.

"At least let me help you wash and dry up," he replied.

"It's fine…." I went to continue before he cut me off.

"No, I insist. You wash and I'll dry."

"You're not going to take no for an answer, are you?" I asked him.

"No, so you might as well give in now," He said with a grin.

After helping with the drying up, I made Chris go and sit in the living room while I made the coffee. Walking in, I found Chris sitting on the sofa looking up at the pictures of my parents and brother. Placing the coffee mugs down on the table in front of him, I took a seat in the armchair to the side.

"I didn't realise you had a brother, Jess. I assume it is your brother as you look so similar."

"Yes, it's my brother. Not many people do know. He left about eight years ago, before my mum died and dad moved away. You probably weren't even living in the town then."

"No, I moved here about seven and half years ago, just before you bought the coffee shop actually. I got to meet both your parents, though. Your mum was a wonderful lady." He picked up his coffee and looked over to me. "Sorry, didn't mean to put a dampener on the evening."

"It's fine, Chris, I know there are many people still living here that knew my Mum and will remind me of it. It's nice to know she made that kind of impression," I said with a meek smile.

"Where is your brother now?" he asked.

"He moved over to America with his fiancé. They are due to get married later this year. Dad and I are hoping to get out there, but it will depend on if I can get someone to look after the shop for me. It's been five years since I have had a break, and working seven days a week is starting to take its toll. Really, I don't know what I would do without Maddie. She helps me so much."

"She is a lovely girl; I am sure if you asked, she might be able to help you out a bit more."

"Well, I'll just wait and see. I've a while yet."

Noticing that Chris had looked at his watch, I looked up at my clock and noticed it was nearly nine o'clock. Usually by now I was getting ready to tuck myself up in bed. However, with Chris around, I thought it would be rude to ask him to leave; especially as it was me that had asked him around in the first place.

As if sensing my predicament, Chris put down his cup and turned to me.

"Well, it is getting late and we both have to be up early, so if you don't mind, I'm going to head off for the long way home," he said laughing.

"Not a problem at all. I wouldn't want you to be late travelling all that way next door. Thank you for your help tonight and for the company."

"It's me who should be thanking you for a lovely meal, far better than a ding meal anytime. If you're not careful, I'll keep finding reasons to come around just for food," he laughed.

Laughing back, I followed him to the door as he went to leave.

"Don't forget to lock the door behind me, and I'll see you bright and early for my latte and pastry."

"See you in the morning, Chris, and yes, I'll lock the door."

With that, Chris left and I shut and locked the door behind me. Walking back into the living room, I picked up the coffee mugs and went back into the kitchen. Washing them both up, I left them on the sink to dry and then headed to the bedroom to get some much-needed sleep.

Stepping through my bedroom door I felt the same uneasiness I had earlier in the evening. Something just didn't feel right, but looking around again I couldn't see anything untoward. I went to my bed to pick up the pjs I had folded and left there this morning. That was when it hit me. The pyjamas were not there! Standing there for a second, I recollected everything that I had done this morning before walking out the house.

It was freezing cold and I had thrown back the covers, instantly regretting it. I went to the bathroom, brushed my teeth, had a shower, and washed my hair. Walking back into the bedroom, I got dressed and then folded my pjs and put them on my pillow ready for tonight. I remembered doing it.And, I was a creature of habit. Stepping out into the corridor, I went to the laundry basket to check I wasn't mistaken and had put them in there. Opening the lid confirmed exactly what I thought. They were not in there either.

A sense of fear suddenly went through me. Had someone been

in my flat? If so, how did they get in, and why had they only taken my pyjamas? Still worrying about the whole situation, I went around my flat checking every window and the front door again just to make sure that it was locked. Moving back along the corridor I made it back to my room and sat down on the bed. Could I just be imagining this? But if I was, then where were my pyjamas? A yawn escaped my mouth and I realised just how tired my body felt. If I didn't go to bed soon, I was going to be useless in the morning.

Getting up from the bed, I walked over to my chest of drawers and got out a new pair of pyjamas. Changing into them, I climbed into bed and pulled over the covers. Resting my head down on the pillow, thoughts of the missing pair of pjs whirling around my head, I finally allowed sleep to take over my body.

Chapter Five

Jessica

Feeling hot breath on my neck, I stirred in my sleep. Then the soft caress of a hand across my cheek caused me to instinctively lean into it. The breath got closer again as soft lips kissed up my neck and towards my ear, while the hand grazed down my cheek and down softly around my neck. In a second the hand around my neck grasped tightly at my throat and a harsh voice whispered into my ear.

"I'm coming for you!"

Shooting bolt upright in my bed I woke suddenly, gasping for breath, my heart racing, and shaking from head to toe. My hand immediately went to my throat to check it was OK. It was just a nightmare, but it felt so real. It was as though I could still feel the heat from his body, whoever he was. Looking at the clock, I saw it was 4:15. Thinking there wasn't much point trying to rest for 15 minutes, I decided it was probably best just to get up.

Switching off the alarm, I threw the covers off and was pleased to feel the warmth in the room. Thank God for Chris, I thought to myself as I picked up the clothes on the floor to put into the washing basket. Stepping into the corridor, I thought about the nightmare. It must have just been because of the missing pyjamas that my mind was just working overtime.

Opening the lid to the laundry basket, I went to throw in the clothes, but happened to look down before I did. Having to check twice, I couldn't believe what I was seeing, the missing pyjamas were currently staring up at me from the basket. Standing there unable to move, I went through the same routine as I had last night when I found the pjs were missing. Talking to myself I said, "OK, so I checked the pillows, under the pillows, walked out, and checked this basket, and they were nowhere to be found!"

Was I going mad? Knowing that answering myself was even worse than talking to myself, I just made an involuntary laugh escaping my lips. They can't just disappear and reappear like that; there must be a valid explanation, one that I really wanted to find out.

Frustrated, I knew I had to get ready for my day and would have to solve this mystery later.

Allowing myself some extra minutes in the shower, I allowed the stress and worry of the nightmare to wash away like the hot water running over my body. That was exactly what I had to remember, it was just a dream. Dreams can't hurt you, perhaps make you slightly mad, but physically they couldn't hurt you.

Turning off the shower, I wrapped myself in my towel and headed back to my bedroom to get dressed. I pulled on my now trademark jeans and T shirt and went to the kitchen for my first cup of coffee for the day. I placed a pod in my coffee machine and went to get my mug from the drainer where I had left it before going to bed.

Nothing. My mug was not there. The one Chris had used sat there on the draining board, but my favourite mug was gone.

My brother gave it to me as a birthday present not long before he left. It simply said, "The World's Best Little Sister." I could buy one anywhere, but it wouldn't be the same. I opened the cupboard just to check, but it wasn't there. What the hell was going on? Was I truly going mad? My pjs had disappeared last night, I was one hundred percent sure of that, and they reappear today. Now, my mug goes missing and I know I left it here.

I got another mug from the cupboard and made myself a coffee. Today was going to be an awfully long day if the first hour was anything to go by. I grabbed the coffee and headed out of my flat to go down to the shop. I knew Chris would be there soon, so I needed to get myself into gear and ready for the day.

Thinking to myself as I walked down the stairs, I really hoped Maddie would be in the shop today, since I needed to talk to someone about what the hell was going on. Hopefully, she would be able to make some sense of it all and explain to me. Unlocking the back door to the shop, I turned on the lights and quickly put everything in the oven for the day.

I started to make a Hazelnut Latte for Chris and bagged up a couple of pastries, ready for when he came in this morning. Just as I was pouring the coffee into the milk there was a knock on the shop door. Walking over to the door, I looked through it to check who it was. and sure enough it was Chris right when he said he would arrive. Unlocking the door, I opened it and greeted him with a smile.

"Morning, Chris. I was just finishing off your latte for you."

"Morning, Jess. Glad you remembered little old me."

"How could I forget my favourite neighbour?" I replied, chuckling at him.

"I know, I'm pretty unforgettable, aren't I?" He replied, wiggling his eyebrows up and down.

Looking at him with a smile, I just rolled my eyes and replied,

"Conceited much?"

Chris looked at me and just laughed. "Aww, you love me really, don't you, babe? Thanks for a lovely evening last night, Jess. I know it was nothing, but it was nice just to spend some time with another human being and not just be on my own."

Standing there for a second I took in what he said. He had called me babe, yet again. Why would he do that? Was he hitting on me? I know he was making a joke, at least I thought he was. But for two days in a row he used the same phrase. Lost in my thoughts for a moment I hadn't realised Chris had been talking to me.

"Jess. Jess, are you OK?" he asked, pulling me out of my thoughts.

"Oh, sorry, Chris. I was just thinking about something. Yes, I'm OK, and you are more than welcome for last night. I admit it was nice to have someone to talk to. It kind of made me remember the times my brother had been around. We would sit talking for hours."

"You miss him, don't you?" Chris asked.

"Sometimes, yes. Especially when something I do reminds me of him. Most of the time I'm too busy to even care, which sounds terrible, but unfortunately is the truth."

"Well, if you ever need some company or just a good chat, you know I'm only next door."

"Thanks, Chris. I appreciate it," I replied with a slight hesitation in my voice. Something wasn't quite right with Chris this morning, but I couldn't put my finger on what it was. Since I was also feeling on edge, it could just be my imagination. Walking around the counter, I placed the lid on his coffee and passed it over to him, along with his pastries. "Was there anything else for you today?"

"I would love some soup if you have any. I can warm it up at work."

"I do have some chicken and veg soup, actually." I walked out to the back to get it ready for him. I poured a portion of soup into a takeaway container and brought it back out to Chris. "Did you want a roll as well?"

"That would be great," he said, and I put a roll in a bag.

"There you go. I hope you enjoy it."

"Thanks," he said, passing me the money. "I Hope that's enough. If not, let me know and I will pop in later. If it is too much, keep the change." He started walking to the door and turned to speak, but I cut him off before he could say anything.

"Door will be locked as soon as you walk out," I said with a smile.

"Good girl! See you later, Jess."

"Have a good one, Chris," I said as I closed the door behind him and locked it.

Was I imagining things with Chris? He had never been so friendly to me before. Sure, he was friendly and would do anything for anyone, but just lately he seemed to be overly friendly, with the "babe" and our chatting last night. Maddie really needed to be here today. I had to talk. I was really starting to think I was going mad.

I went to the back room to go about my normal morning routine of cooking the pastries and rolls, and making sure I had got cakes out of the freezer so they could defrost. One day I would get extra staff in so I could make my own cakes everyday, but now that just couldn't happen. During the summer I was lucky enough to have a local housewife who loved to bake. She would often cook umpteen cupcakes for me to sell and I would share the profits with her. During the winter however, it wasn't worth it as they hardly sold.

I placed the soup into two large slow cookers to warm up. Having found them in the depths of the kitchen, I knew they would be ideal for keeping the soup warm during the day. All I had to do was put it into either a bowl or a container whenever anyone ordered it. Tomorrow it would be a good old-fashioned leek and potato soup, warming, filling and would make any Vegan or Vegetarians happy as well. Plus, I already had everything I needed for that. Although, thinking about it, I didn't tend to come across many vegetarians in our small town, except for the odd passer-by.

A loud knock at the front door pulled me from my thoughts. I looked up at the clock and saw it would be Mr. Duncan in for his usual coffees. I walked to the front and started the coffee machine for two lattes and then walked to the front door to see Mr. Duncan standing there. Unlocking and opening the door, I greeted him in my usual cheery manner.

"Good morning, Mr. Duncan. How are you this morning?"

"Good morning, Jess. Mabel and I are both well, thank you. And how are you, my dear? You look tired this morning. Is everything OK?" he asked, the concern clear on his face.

Mr. and Mrs. Duncan always looked out for me and were more like an aunt and uncle to me than just neighbours. I loved them both for that. They were also very friendly with my Dad and Edith, which was always good.

"I'm OK, Mr. Duncan. I just had a restless night's sleep and a bit of a bad dream this morning. Nothing I can't handle, though."

"Well, you make sure you are looking after yourself, my dear. I wouldn't want you making yourself ill. If you ever need anything, you know where to find us. Anyway, I understand that Mabel has ordered two bowls of your lovely soup for lunch today, along with our usual sandwiches."

"Yes, she has. I'm sure you are going to love it. You can also let her know that it's leek and potato soup tomorrow if you are interested."

"I can tell you now that we will have two bowls tomorrow as well. That is my favourite, well apart from oxtail soup, but that is such a pain to make from scratch, so we usually just buy it in a tin. I think that is the right amount, from what Mabel said, but if it isn't let me know and I will pop some more around when I collect our lunch."

"Perfect as always, Mr. Duncan. There are your lattes and pastries." I handed over his drinks and the usual pain au chocolat.

"Thank you, my dear. I will see you later for lunch." And with that, Mr. Duncan turned and left the shop.

Quickly I went to the back and got the trays of pastries and put the next batch into the oven. Checking the soup, I could see that it was starting to warm up nicely and would be ready in time for the lunchtime special. Walking over to my chalk menu board I wrote up the special soup of the day. Going through my regular routine had helped take the creepy events of last night off my mind.

Switching on the filter coffee machine, I got the first brew of the day on the go. Once it was ready, I would pour myself a cup to get me through the first part of the morning. As I was getting it ready, I heard the bell go on the door to indicate there was a customer in the shop. Turning around, I saw that it was Tyler.

Tyler worked for the Private Investigator around the corner. He and Jayden quite often came into the shop to get lunch for themselves and the other guys at the firm. They were both nice guys, a little young for my liking, but were always polite and happy when they came in.

"Morning, Tyler. You are early this morning. What can I do to help you today?"

"Morning, Jess. Yeah, early start today. Got a meeting with the boss before I head off to a job. I need a coffee. You know I'm not a morning person," he said with a chuckle.

"Well, I guess so, since I've never seen you before about 12:00! So just a latte for you?" I asked.

"Hey, I'm feeling adventurous this morning. Can I have one gingerbread latte for me, and I best get Mace a latte as well, or he would never forgive me. Could I also grab a couple of pastries and can I collect a tuna mayo baguette on my way back?"

"Of course. I will have it ready for when you get back. I will make it once you leave just in case your meeting is quick."

"Thanks, Jess. You are a lifesaver."

"Who's Mace, anyway? I never heard you guys talk about him when you come in?"

"You must have met Mason. I'm sure he came in to get lunch yesterday, or maybe the day before? Anyway, he is Jayden's older brother and basically the boss. He's OK, just needs to chill out a bit occasionally."

"We all probably need to do that," I said as I finished off the lattes and placed them in front of him. "That one's the gingerbread one, just so you know. What pastries did you want?"

"Oh, just a couple of croissants will be fine, thanks."

Picking two croissants up, I placed them in the bag and put them on the counter next to the drinks.

"There you go," I said as I took the money he was handing me. I rang it into the till and passed him the change.

"When did you start serving soup?" he asked as he took the change.

"First day today. I thought I would see how it went."

"Well, make sure there is enough for us all on Monday. I'm sure the guys would all like to have something hot for lunch."

"Will do, Tyler. Have a good day."

"You too, Jess." With that, he turned and walked out the shop.

So, the chicken and salad baguette guy finally had a name. Mason King. Although Tyler hadn't told me his surname, I knew it was King as the business was called King Brothers Investigations. Therefore Jayden and Mason must be the King brothers who owned it. Now I had a name to use in my fantasy.

Chapter Six

Mason

It was just past 7:00, and I was already in the office. Usually, I wouldn't get into the office until at least 8:00, but Tyler was due to go for his interview today at 10:30, so I needed to speak to him before he went. As it was so early in the morning, I decided not to leave Monty on his own for the whole day and had brought him with me to the office.

Monty had often come with me to the office. He would just go and sit on his bed in the corner and would only go for a wander if one of the guys walked past or called him. Jayden would often take him out for a walk at lunchtime. He would say that it was so he could get some fresh air and allow Monty to do "his business," but I was sure he was just doing it to attract the girls, and believe me, I knew Monty did that.

I was sitting in my office looking through some paperwork when I heard the front door open. I looked up and saw Tyler walk into my office complete with coffee and a bag, which I assumed had a pastry in it.

"Morning, Mace. I brought you a latte and croissant. Jayden warned me that you don't fare too well at this time of the morning without caffeine," he said, laughing at his own comment.

"Oh, he did, did he? I function perfectly well with or without coffee at this time of the morning, but I am not going to turn it down, so thank you, Tyler."

"So, are you all ready for your interview today with Mr. Jarvis?" I asked Tyler.

"Yes, I have my suit in the other room. You know how much I hate them, so I wanted to be in it for the shortest time possible. I know everything about the business, so if I'm asked anything, I should be able to answer it with ease. Unless there is something else you think I should know?"

"Well, you already know the kind of questions that you're going to be asked, so there's no need to go over them, plus I wouldn't have the foggiest idea what you were going on about anyway. Once you've had your interview, Mr. Jarvis is going to take you around the area in which you'll be working to introduce you to everyone. Have a good look around and make sure you say hello to them all. Mr. Jarvis is going to do this with all the interviewees, although he did say the others wouldn't normally get the job, so it's not as though you are costing someone a chance at work."

"OK, is there anything else that I need to know about, Mace?"

"No, I think that's everything. Are you going to come back here when you're done, or are you going straight home from there?"

"Not sure yet, I will give you a call once I have finished the interview. If anyone hears me, it will be just like any normal person would do if they had come out of an interview. Anyway, I best get changed and get on my way. Got to pick up my lunch from Jessica's before I get on my way."

"If you're going to Jessica's, could you please order me a baguette and a latte, please. Let her know I will be there about 12:30, but will have Monty with me so I will have to wait outside."

"Will do, Mace."

"OK, have a safe journey and I'll speak to you later. Thanks again for the coffee."

"No problem, Mace."

With that Tyler left my office and went to get ready for the day. I looked over at the clock on my office wall and saw it was just coming up for 8:30. Sipping my coffee, I decided that it would be a good time to take Monty out for a short walk. He loved being at the office, but could be a bit of a distraction at times, so I only tended to bring him here when I was on my own as he would just curl up in a ball and sleep.

Standing up from my chair, I called over to him. "Come on boy, let's get some fresh air." He immediately lifted his head and ears and got up to trot over to me. As we were in town he would have to be on a lead. I worried there were too many people and cars around for him to get involved with and hurt.

"Yes, I know boy, you don't like the lead, but you know you have to have it around here," I said as I clipped the lead onto his collar and started to walk out of the office with him. Walking out the front door to the office, I locked it behind me and headed into town. It was a short walk to the high street, which we went through to get to the park on the other side of the town.

It was around a thirty-minute walk, but it allowed me to gather my thoughts and I would often do this even if Monty wasn't with me. The business was doing well, but the stress it put me under sometimes was unbelievable. Jayden and Brandon were great at running things day to day, but all the finances were left up to me. We weren't broke by any means, but I always worried that costs would spiral out of hand and we would go under like so many other investigation firms had before.

One thing was for sure, if things did get bad then one of the offices would have to go. As I owned the one here outright, I would probably have to keep this and just rent a room somewhere daily for meetings in London. It was something we had considered as a group when I left to come down here, but at present we could afford it, so there was no need to change.

As I walked past the small parade of shops, I saw Mrs. Duncan stepping out from her shop. Mr. and Mrs. Duncan had lived here all their lives and were always willing to help everyone. And in Mrs. Duncan's case, sometimes her version of helping was to interfere and match make. Several times she had tried to introduce me to one of the ladies in the town. Even though she knew everything that I had gone through, she had made it her mission to get me settled down with a lovely local lady.

When I thought about it, it was quite sweet, and one day she may catch me with my guard down and I'll give in. However, that day was not today.

"Well, hello there, Monty. And how are we today? You're such a good boy, aren't you?" Mrs. Duncan addressed Monty before me, which always tends to happen.

"Good morning, Mrs. Duncan. How are you this morning?"

"Good morning, Mason. Please call me Mabel. Mrs. Duncan is so formal."

"My parents brought me up to respect those older than me, so I will not apologise for being so formal, Mrs. Duncan," I said with a smile.

"Always the smooth gentleman, Mason. You sound like Jess in the coffee shop. She insists on Mr. and Mrs. Duncan for the exact same reason." "Talking of Jess, do you speak to her much?"

"Actually, no. I think I have only been in her shop once. The guys always go in there and get me a coffee or lunch. Why do you ask, Mrs. Duncan? Are you trying a bit of matchmaking again?"

"Well, while I wouldn't be averse to you two together," she smiled, "I was actually a bit worried about her. Well, Mr. Duncan was, actually. She has been very jumpy lately and looks as though she hasn't been getting much sleep."

"I'm not really sure there is much I can do about that, I'm afraid. As I said, I don't really know her that well. Why don't you have a chat with her, and if she thinks we can be of help at Kings then please send her in to see us."

"Thank you, Mason. We appreciate that. I will let you get on with your walk. You look after yourself and that handsome Monty of yours as well."

"We will. See you later, Mrs. Duncan. And say hello to Mr. Duncan for me as well."

"I will do," she said, as I continued down the road to the park.

When I arrived at the park, seeing it was empty, I finally allowed Monty to go off his lead. He absolutely loved being off lead and I knew that he would not get himself into trouble here. I walked around the outside of the park, with Monty running off and back in his usual manner. Up here I could think. It was like me going for a walk on the downs near my home.

I wandered around the park, just allowing random thoughts to come and go, one of which was my upcoming visit to my parents. It was the same thing every week. Mum would ask if I had found myself a nice girlfriend, how she wasn't getting any younger and would like to have grandchildren while she was young enough to enjoy them.

She didn't understand what Cassandra had done to me. Mum thought I could just forget and move on, but it wasn't as easy as that. Sure, I knew that people did have healthy and loving relationships. My parents were testimony to that. However, I spent most days seeing the worst kind of relationships, the liars, cheaters, and manipulators. So why would I risk putting myself through that all over again?

At least Dad understood, probably because he was a man, and although he loved Mum, he understood that men don't really have the kind of need that a woman does. When he saw things getting too much for me, he would suggest we go for a walk. He was the only person that had seen me cry, and the only person I would cry in front of. Even my brother didn't see how much Cassandra's actions had hurt me.

Sitting down on the bench at one end of the park, Monty came rushing over to me and placed his head in my lap. Always the loyal companion, he knew when I needed him and would immediately be there by my side. As I sat there looking at the changing colours of the trees, I wondered whether my Mum and Mrs. Duncan were right? Was it time for me to move on? It had been nearly three years and even though I was only in my early thirties, I wasn't getting any younger. The thoughts went around in my head until a cold wet nose on my hand brought me back to reality.

"Sorry, boy, was I ignoring you? Come, let's get back to the office. Perhaps we can meet someone on the way back, although I am not sure there's anyone here who would see me for anything other than a wealthy business owner." I chuckled to myself, thinking I was going mad having a normal conversation with my dog. I really needed to find myself someone.

We walked across the park, and I put Monty back on the lead. Walking back through the town, we headed back to the office to catch up on some work before lunchtime came. One bonus of being the boss was I could keep whatever hours I liked; I always had my phone with me so if anyone wanted me, they could get hold of me easily.

As I approached the office, I saw a black truck driving towards town. Strange, we don't usually see that kind of vehicle at this time of year. In the summer, we always had strange cars driving through town. But during the autumn and winter months it was just the locals. Standing there for a moment, I watched it drive off into the distance. Thinking it must be someone lost and following their SatNav, I turned back towards the building.

Stepping back into the office, I decided I would get some work done and leave the office at lunchtime and work from home. I always got more work done there anyway, usually because I would carry on working until late. If I stayed at the office, I usually finished at 5:00 and then just went home to relax. Perhaps I should stay at the office more as I would have more time to relax?

After making sure to check that Monty had enough water to drink, I sat down at my desk and started to work through the emails I had received and my work for the day.

Chapter Seven

Jessica

I t had been a normal morning with people coming and going. Maddie was sitting in her usual place, and after the lunchtime rush I was going to sit down with her for a while and explain everything that had happened over the past couple of days. I just had one more order to get ready for pick up. When Tyler had popped back to get his lunch, he had asked me to get a baguette ready for Mason to pick up at 12.30.

Back in the kitchen, I got a granary baguette with chicken and salad ready for when Mason King turned up. Wrapping it up and then cutting it into two, I placed them into a bag ready for him to collect. Thinking it best not to add fuel to Maddie's fire regarding 'chicken & salad baguette man', I hadn't told her that I now not only knew his name, but that he would be back again this lunchtime. She would only tell me that I should be going for it, that I wasn't getting any younger, and should settle down before my biological clock went into overdrive.

I stepped out from the back to see Maddie still sitting in her window seat working away on her laptop. All my orders were ready now. The only thing I had to do was pour out two bowls of soup for Mr. and Mrs. Duncan when they came in to collect their order. Standing at the coffee machine I started to make five lattes, two for the Duncans, one for Mason, and then one for Maddie and myself. If I couldn't benefit from owning the coffee shop and having a latte every now and then, what was the point?

Walking over to Maddie, I placed down two lattes, ready for us to sit down and have a chat when the door opened, and Mr. Duncan walked in. Walking over to the counter, I finished off the two lattes for him.

"Good afternoon to you, Mr. Duncan. There are your lattes. I will just go out back to get your soup and sandwiches," I said as Mr. Duncan walked up to the counter.

"Thank you, Jess, my dear."

Walking back into the kitchen, I poured their soup into containers and picked up the two sandwiches, and walked back into the shop.

"There you go, Mr. Duncan. I hope you both enjoy the soup."

"I'm sure we will, Jess, and please do not stay too late tonight. You still look tired and we are both worried about you. If you need a day off, Mabel would be happy to look after the shop for you."

"Thank you for the offer, Mr. Duncan, but I couldn't ask that of you both. You have enough on your hands running your business, without looking after mine as well. Don't worry about me. I will be fine."

"Well, the offer is there if you ever need it. Have a good day, and I will see you bright and early in the morning, my dear."

"Will do, and see you in the morning," I replied as Mr. Duncan left the shop. As he was shutting the door, I heard him say hello to Mason King, so I walked to the back to pick up his baguette and then went and finished his latte.

As I walked back towards the front door, I caught Maddie staring out the window, obviously looking at Mason. I walked past her smiling and went out the door. Two steps out and I was greeted by an excited spaniel. I guess he was the reason why I had to bring the lunch out to Mason. Tyler hadn't told me that, just that he wouldn't be able to come into the shop.

"Hello, gorgeous. And what's your name, boy?" I said to the spaniel as he obediently sat down at my feet allowing me to stroke him. Feeling a presence close by, I looked up and found myself staring into the most piercing set of hazel eyes glancing down at me.

Catching my breath, I spoke "Sorry, I didn't mean to get him into trouble."

"Monty, his name is Monty, and he isn't in any trouble. Quite the opposite in fact. He hardly ever sits like that when he encounters new people. He's usually a complete pain, so he must really like you. I'm Mason King, by the way. I'm not sure we have ever really been introduced."

"I'm Jessica Davis, but everyone calls me Jess." I held out my hand, which he took. "It's a pleasure to finally meet you since I've been making your lunch every Monday for what seems like ages."

Mason laughed, "I guess Jayden and Tyler have told you all about me, then?"

"Oh, yes, they told me how much of a terrible boss you were, and that if they didn't get your lunch from me then you would sack them!" I tried to keep a straight face. Unfortunately, the look of shock on Mason's face just about did me in and I burst into laughter.

"I'm sorry. They didn't really say any of that, but the look on your face was amazing. Tyler doesn't mention you much, and Jayden just says that you need to get out more, and that one day he will send you for the lunch order. However, now that I realise you are the oldest, I'm sure that's not going to happen."

I passed him his latte and baguette. "There you go, Mason. Tyler paid for it, so you don't have to worry."

He smiled, taking the drink and bag. "Thank you, Jess, and please call me Mace. Mason sounds far too formal from your lips."

I glanced away, feeling myself starting to blush, and to make matters worse, Mason had noticed.

"Sorry, I didn't mean to make you blush."

"It's OK. I'm just not used to compliments from handsome strangers, especially ones with such a gorgeous dog as a pet. Isn't that right, Monty?"

With that I got a small bark and a tail wag from Monty, and a laugh from Mason.

"You definitely have him wrapped around your finger. He has never replied to anyone talking to him except me and the guys in the office. We are definitely going to have to spend more time here, aren't we, boy?" Mason gained another barked reply from Monty.

"Thank you for this, Jess. I really appreciate it," he smiled at me.

"You're welcome Mace and next time I'll make sure I have a little treat for Monty." I gave Monty a pat on the head. "I'll let you get on. Hopefully, we can speak again soon."

"I hope so too, Jess." With a final "woof" from Monty, they headed back down the road to his office.

As I went to turn round to go back into the shop, I noticed a person on the other side of the road. It was a guy, dressed all in black, wearing a hat and sunglasses. He seemed out of place for the small town, almost sinister looking. He held my gaze for a few seconds and then walked off up towards the park. I felt a chill run up my spine. This really wasn't helping after the morning I had.

Trying to brush off the feeling, I went to walk back into the shop and caught Maddie smiling from ear to ear. She had obviously been watching the whole interaction between Mason and myself, and I wasn't going to hear the last of this.

As soon as I stepped through the door, Maddie started with the questions.

"So, what is his name? Where does he work? Did you get his number? Is that ....." Immediately I cut her off.

"Maddie, enough already. Let me answer one question at a time. His name is Mason King, and he owns King Brothers Investigation Services with his brother Jayden. You quite often see Jayden and Tyler in here. In fact I seem to remember you saying that Tyler was cute," I said, knowing that would shut her up for a short period of time at least.

"I didn't get his number, but seeing as his dog Monty and I hit it off, I suspect he will be popping by more often," I said with an obvious smile on my face. "Anyway, I didn't want to talk about me and your imaginary relationship with Mr. Chicken Salad Baguette man. I really need some advice, Maddie. Some really strange things have been happening, and I don't know if I am going mad or should be worried."

For the rest of the afternoon, I explained to Maddie everything that had happened over the past couple of days, in between serving customers and getting everything ready for the next day. From the missing PJs, Chris calling me babe on two occasions, and then the PJs reappearing this morning, and the missing mug.

"So, what do you think, Maddie. Am I going mad, or do you think

I should be worried?" I asked her.

"Well, something doesn't seem right, so I don't think you're going mad. If something else happens then you have got to go to the police. As for Chris, you know he was extremely friendly to me at one time. I found him creepy. He is nearly ten years older than me, then suddenly, he just stopped coming around. He still says hello and is polite, but that is it. To be honest, I'm quite happy about it, but not if he is now starting on you. Perhaps you should start going out with Mason, and then he might leave you alone?"

"Well, while I'm glad you don't think I am going mad, I am not so sure about going out with Mason."

"Why not?"

"Because I really don't think I'm his type. He is handsome and drop dead gorgeous. Even his eyes are an amazing hazel colour. Look at me, plain Jane, twenty-eight years old He wouldn't even look at me twice, let alone go out with me."

"What are you talking about? He definitely looked at you twice while you were talking out there. The look in his eyes when you were talking was real, believe me."

"Well, I suppose we will just have to wait and see. If he asks me out, then I won't say no, OK."

Looking up at the clock I noticed that it was already 4:30. I had to finish everything off, and get ready for the morning.

"Right, I have to get back to it if I want to get finished and in bed early tonight. Mr. Duncan was right in one respect. I am feeling really tired."

"Why don't you close early tonight? No-one usually comes in after 5:00. It will do you some good to get a good night's rest. If anything else happens give me a call, and then call the police."

"Perhaps you're right. I will close up early tonight. There is some soup left. Would you like some for dinner tonight?"

"That would be great, thank you. Just make sure there is enough left for you as well."

"There is more than enough left for both of us."

Walking out back, I grabbed a container and filled it with soup for Maddie to take with her and placed a roll in a bag. Stepping back into the shop, I walked over to Maddie and placed the soup and roll down on the table.

"There you go, hunny. I can't have you going hungry now, can I?"

"Thank you, Jess. You're the best. I don't know how I would survive without you sometimes."

"I'm sure you would survive quite well, but you're welcome anyway."

"Right, well, I will let you close up and get home for some rest. If anything else strange happens then just call the police, OK?"

"I will do, and thank you for believing me and for not thinking I'm mad."

"Anytime. We girls have to stick together, you know."

With that she packed away her laptop and gathered up the soup and roll and made her way out of the shop. I stood there for a while, just taking in the silence. I needed this, just a few moments of quiet time to get my thoughts together.

Walking over to the door, I changed the open sign to closed and locked the shop door. Looking out the window, I noticed the same guy that was across the road earlier, staring over at the shop. This time however, he was standing next to the black truck. What the hell was going on? I really needed to get a grip on myself and get some rest. I was probably just worrying over nothing after this morning's goings on. I walked away from the shop front, taking one last glance over my shoulder. The space where the truck had been was now empty. Was I going mad? I was sure I hadn't imagined it. Spending the next thirty minutes in the shop cleaning up and getting ready for the following day, I looked at the clock and decided to call it a day at 5:45.

Locking the shop up behind me, I went up the stairs to my flat and opened the door. As soon as I walked through the door I noticed that there was an unusual smell in the flat, one that I was sure I had smelled before. It smelled like a man's aftershave, but I couldn't put my finger on when I had smelled it.

Placing my keys in the bowl on the kitchen table, I put the container of soup I had brought up with me into the microwave ready to heat up for dinner later. Deciding I would have a shower first, I walked out of the kitchen and my eye was immediately drawn to my photos above the fireplace. They had all been rearranged, and I knew it wasn't by me. Thinking back to the night before, I tried to recollect if Chris had moved any. I know we discussed them, but he was sitting down all the time, so it wasn't then.

Deciding to check if my mug had reappeared, I walked back into the kitchen and saw that it was still missing. This was starting to get worrying. Who was coming into my flat, and more to the point, how were they getting in? I couldn't take this anymore. I didn't feel safe in my own home, so I decided to take Maddie's advice and call the police.

Chapter Eight

Jessica

It had been two days since I called the police and basically been laughed at. They didn't think that I was in any danger, so they weren't going to investigate. They didn't seem to care that someone had obviously been in my flat and took items, put them back, or moved them. They basically said unless I was physically attacked or threatened there wasn't much they could do.

Since then, I had items of clothing taken, including underwear, pictures of me and my friends in school and college, and a set of my chef's knives. That was the most worrying thing to me, that someone was going around with lethal weapons in their hands.

So, thanks to that I was now sitting in my bedroom at 3:00 a.m. worrying if the next time someone came into my flat, they would attack me. Everything had been quiet for twenty-four hours and nothing had been taken or moved, so I was hoping that was the end of things. However, I had a feeling that things were about to take a turn for the worse. Something had woken me about an hour ago, but I was too worried to leave my bedroom to find out.

Sitting in my bed, I listened for any noise that could indicate there was someone in my flat. All was quiet, so quiet you could hear a pin drop. Well, I was awake now, so I might as well get out of bed and get ready for the day. Hesitantly, I got out of bed and headed to my bedroom door. Opening it, I peeked around the corner. Nothing. All was quiet.

Venturing into the living room, I looked up on the mantelpiece. Someone had been in my flat again. The picture of my brother and me was missing. Why would someone take that, along with the mug my brother had bought me. Standing there for a moment, I wondered if they were targeting items relating to my brother and me. It was not making any sense.

As it was still early, I decided to make myself a mug of coffee before getting ready for the day. I walked into the kitchen to turn the coffee machine on. As I was waiting for my coffee to finish brewing, I stood there in a daze just thinking everything through. Going over everything that happened in my head, I still couldn't fathom why some of the items being taken had something to do with my brother.

Sean had left town eight years ago to start a new life in America with Nicola. Why would someone be so interested in him now? Standing there quietly contemplating everything, I heard a door open and close. It must be Chris, I thought to myself. He would be the only one up and about at this time of the morning. Footsteps came towards the front door. One problem with these flats was they weren't very soundproof, and you could hear almost everything that went on outside the flat.

Standing there for a minute, I expected a knock on the front door, and was just about to walk towards it when I heard the footsteps trail away and assumed Chris had left for his day. Strange, why would he walk to the front of my flat? The stairs were in a totally different direction. I mentally shrugged, putting it down to Chris thinking better of knocking on my door at 4:00 in the morning.

Hearing the heat kick in was a reminder of how lucky I was to have Chris as a neighbour. I put down my coffee and went to have my shower and get ready for the day.

On Saturday morning things didn't usually pick up until around 9:00 a.m., as most people had the luxury of two days off. Unfortunately, I wasn't one of them. Choosing the life of a coffee shop owner, I hadn't really thought that it was a seven day a week job. The weekends were my busiest times during the autumn and winter, and being that it was September, the residents of Kings View would come in droves for breakfast on a Saturday morning.

I had just served the umpteenth coffee and croissant, thank god for the freezer and extra pastries I had made during the week, when Maddie walked into the shop. She would often come in on a weekend and help me entertain customers, making sure they were all happy and had everything they needed.

I only tended to wait on tables on the weekend and that was only because I had Maddie around to help. The customers loved her, and I thought back to what Chris said the other night. Perhaps I should ask her to help out around the shop. I know she did it anyway, but I was sure she could use at least a weekend job to help pay the bills. Her student loan would only go so far.

Deciding that I would have a chat with her once the lunchtime rush was over, I continued to make the latte and cappuccino for the table I was currently serving. Placing them on the tray along with two pain au chocolats, I walked over to the table and placed them down.

"Thank you, Jess, much appreciated. We don't know what we would do without you on a Saturday morning; it really is the highlight of our week," the old man of the couple said.

"You're welcome. I'm glad I can give you some happiness each week." They were regulars in the shop and had been coming every Saturday morning for the past couple of years. The funny thing was that during all that time I hadn't asked their names, and it seemed a bit strange to ask them now.

Smiling at them both as I turned to walk away, I noticed a figure standing in the doorway, but not coming through. Looking closely, I saw that it was Mason. He never came here on a Saturday. Hell, he never came here at all. Looking down, I noticed the reason why he was not entering the shop. He had Monty with him. Turning to Maddie, I said, "Maddie, could you just keep an eye on the shop while I help Mason? He has Monty with him, so can't come in the shop."

"Of course I can," she replied with a waggle of her eyebrows.

Rolling my eyes at her, I turned and walked towards the door, opened it, and greeted Mason with a smile.

"Hey, Mace," I said, remembering not to call him Mason as it was 'too formal.' "What can I do for you and the gorgeous Monty this morning?"

"Hi, Jess. We were just in town, and I thought I could grab a latte and croissant from you if that is OK?"

"Of course you can. Give me five minutes and I'll bring it out for you." Reaching down to Monty I spoke to him. "I might also have a little something for you as well, boy. Take a seat, Mace, and I'll be back in a sec." Monty barked his appreciation as I turned to hear Mason chuckling behind me.

Walking back into the shop, I saw Maddie had already started making a latte for Mason and was smiling away to herself.

"What?" I asked trying not to smile back at the cheesy grin she was currently giving me.

"Nothing," she replied. "I have a latte ready for Mason, and there is a croissant in a bag on the counter."

"How did you know what he ordered?" I asked her.

"Oh, just a hunch."

Chuckling, I walked to the back to get a couple of the biscuits I had made for Monty. Knowing I quite often had customers sitting outside with their dogs, especially in the summer, I looked up a dog friendly biscuit recipe and made some last night before I went to bed. Secretly, I was hoping that Mason would bring Monty back so I could try them out on him, but I knew that with the lovely autumn weather we were having, I was bound to get one customer here over the weekend with a dog.

I picked up two biscuits, one for now and one Mason could take with him; I walked back to the counter and picked up the latte and croissant that Maddie had gotten ready. Ignoring the comment that was about to come from Maddie's lips, I walked back out to the front of the shop to take them to Mason.

Opening the door, I found him sitting at one of the tables with a very obedient Monty sitting by his side. Monty's ears immediately pricked up as I stepped outside, and I could see his tail wagging furiously. Placing the drink and pastry down on the table, I took a seat next to Monty, who immediately got up and sat right in front of me.

Mason looked down at Monty and laughed.

"I can see where your loyalty really lies now, can't I, boy? Clearly, with anyone that has treats for you," he said, shaking his head.

With a small woof, Monty looked at Mason and then turned back to me, ears up and tail wagging.

"Is it OK for him to have one of these biscuits? I made them last night. They're dog friendly."

"I don't know, what do you think, Monty?" Mason asked, gaining a woof in reply from Monty. Laughing, he said, "Well, I guess that's an OK then."

"I guess it was." I gave Monty a biscuit, which he quickly devoured.

"You know, he will want to come here all the time now, don't you?" Mason turned to me and said with a smile on his face.

"I suspect he will, but it's not a problem as I have plenty of biscuits left, and they keep for weeks. I have one here for you to give him later. Don't want to spoil him too much," I said, passing the second biscuit to Mason.

"Thank you." He went to place the biscuit in his pocket, but as he did, his hand briefly touched mine. What I could only describe as a shot of electricity, ran through my hand and my eyes immediately shot up. Mason must have felt it too, as we were now staring into each other's eyes.

Feeling my face immediately turning crimson in embarrassment, I dropped my gaze back down to the table and moved my hand away from where it had been touching his for the past few seconds.

"Jess, I..." Mason started to say when he was cut off by Mrs. Duncan, who had just walked up to the shop.

"Good morning, Mason, Jess. Lovely day, isn't it? I'm just coming round to collect our lunch order for today," she said, walking past and into the shop. This would lead to twenty questions when I walked back in.

"I'd better head in to get Mrs. Duncan's order together," I said with a deflated tone in my voice.

"Yes, I had better be getting off too. Thanks for Monty's biscuits, and here's what I owe you. Just take the change off the lunch bill on Monday," he said, getting up from the chair. "I'll see you around, Jess," he said with a smile. He hesitated for a second as if he wanted to say something, but turned and then headed up the street.

Standing there for a second, I watched him walk up the street. God, he was gorgeous. Did he feel the same way about me though? He couldn't deny he felt that spark too. It was written all over his face. With one last glance down the road at him, I turned to go back in the shop, and on opening the door found Mrs. Duncan and Maddie staring at me. They had obviously been talking because they both went silent as soon as I walked in.

It was then that I realised it was only 11:00 a.m. and far too early for Mrs. Duncan to pick up their lunch order. She had obviously seen Mason and me talking and decided to do a little bit of matchmaking. Either that, or she just wanted some gossip.

"Mrs. Duncan, you're a little early today. I haven't had a chance to get your lunch order ready yet. If you want to have a coffee and wait, I can get it done for you in ten minutes."

"Oh, don't worry about that, my dear. Mr. Duncan can get it at the usual time, but I will have a coffee. Come on, sit down with me and tell me all about you and that scrumptious Mr. King," she said with a beam on her face.

"What? There's nothing to tell. He was just walking by and wanted a coffee and a croissant. He had to wait outside as he had Monty. I had made some dog biscuits, so we were just outside talking. That's it, nothing more to say, really." I felt myself dying with embarrassment inside.

"Hmmm, if you say so. However, the look on his face when I walked up said differently. You two are perfect for each other. I say go for it, you only live once."

Maddie brought us all over a coffee and we sat and chatted for a while about nothing in particular. Feeling quite glad that Mason wasn't brought up again, I didn't think I would be able to hide my feelings for much longer if they carried on. Mason King was definitely a man I could fall for. He was handsome, had a good job, and he was kind to animals, but I hadn't been in any kind of relationship for years. How could I even ask him if he wanted to go out with me? We hardly knew each other. I would just have to settle for the odd moments when he popped into the shop.

Chapter Nine

Mason

Even though I usually had to put up with mum going on about finding a girlfriend, Sunday was my favourite day, and I loved spending time with my parents. Family was always important to me, which is why I tried to spend Sunday each week with Mum and Dad. If I could get Jayden to come along, it was even better, and this was going to be one of those weeks.

However, even though I was looking forward to seeing them, I still had one person on my mind, Jessica. Yesterday, I had purposely gone to the coffee shop to see her. I wanted to get to know her better, perhaps even ask her out. Jayden and Brandon were right. I had to move on with my life, and after spending just those few minutes with Jess, I knew I wanted it to be with her.

Monty loved her, and he was a very good judge of character. The one time he had met Cassandra after we split up, he spent the entire time by my side growling at her. But with Jess, he was happy and interacted with her as if she was a long lost friend, and the fact she went out of her way to make him happy told me everything about her.

Then there was that time when our hands touched, and I know she felt that spark. At that moment, all I wanted to do was grab her into my arms and take her to bed. I have never felt an attraction to anyone like I did in those few short seconds.

Laying there reminiscing about yesterday, I looked over at the clock on my bedside table, 8:30 am. If I wasn't going to be late to Mum and Dad's, I needed to get my arse in gear and get ready for the day. Throwing my covers off of me, Monty immediately jumped up and ran out of the bedroom, ready for breakfast.

"OK, boy. On my way," I said, lifting myself out of bed.

Walking out towards the kitchen, I went to the cupboard to get Monty's food out and placed it in his bowl on the floor. While he stood there eagerly eating his breakfast, I turned on the coffee machine and started a pot brewing. No day could start without a good mug of coffee; Jayden was right on that one respect. I didn't function well without coffee in the morning.

Picking up my phone, I sent a quick text to Jayden to make sure he was up and getting ready to go to Mum and Dad's, knowing if I didn't, he wouldn't make it until early afternoon. Amazingly, I got a message back within seconds saying he was already on his second cup of coffee. Wow, wonders will never cease, I thought to myself.

Walking back into my bedroom, I grabbed a towel from the cupboard and walked into the bathroom. Turning on the shower, I undressed, stepped into the shower and allowed the hot water to cascade over my body. Standing there in the warmth of the water, I allowed my mind to wander to Jess. Thoughts of her standing in front of me, her brunette hair falling across her breasts, had me hard in a matter of seconds.

I imagined her lips touching mine, her body so close I could feel her erect nipples grazing across my skin. Warmth flooded through me and my cock grew harder, if that was even possible. I grabbed it in my hand and started pumping, imagining her soft hand caressing it while we kissed, lost in my thoughts.

Images of her flooded my head as I continued to fist myself, I imagined my hands caressing her breasts, taking her nipple in my mouth and sucking and nipping it between my teeth, rolling the other between my fingers. Hearing the moans coming off her lips as she called out my name, I placed my fingers into her and gently massaged her bud, making her come undone with pleasure in my arms.

In a matter of minutes, I could feel the pleasure building inside me as I continued to pump my cock hard. Within what seemed like seconds, I felt my balls tighten and the ecstasy of my release as I came all over my hand and body. For a moment I felt my legs weaken and had to hold myself up with my free hand resting it on the wall to stop me from falling over.

"Fuck," I said to myself as I came down from my sexual high and picked up my shower gel to clean myself up.

I had never jacked myself off in the shower, thinking about a woman before. That told me everything about Jess. I needed her, wanted her, and I would do everything in my power to make her mine. Turning the shower down as cold as I could bear, I quickly calmed myself down and switched it off to get ready for the day, and it was going to be a long day.

After the shower incident, I got dressed, drank my coffee and headed out with Monty. I sent a quick text to Jayden saying I was on my way to our parents' house and got into the car with Monty settled in the back.

The drive to my parents' was only about thirty minutes to the city of Winchester. They loved the area and had moved down from London about ten years ago while I was still in the forces and Jayden was just completing his training to join the army.

They had a lovely cottage just on the outskirts of the city and spent most of their retirement enjoying the peace and quiet of the surrounding countryside.

Driving up to the cottage at around 10:00, I noticed that Jayden had also arrived and was currently getting out of his car to be greeted by our Mum. Pulling up beside his car, I switched off the engine, got out of my car, and walked around to the back to get Monty out. He loved coming here because my Mum would always spoil him rotten, and I often wondered if he would prefer to live with my parents rather than me at times.

Letting him out of the car, he immediately jumped out and headed straight over to my Mum who bent down to give him his usual stroke hello behind the ears. Walking over to her, I pulled her into a hug and gave her a kiss on the cheek.

"Hi, Mum. How are you?" I asked.

"I am good, thank you. How are you? Still no girlfriend to bring round and see me, I see. You know I want a daughter-in-law to go shopping with, don't you? It would also be nice to have grandbabies before I get too old to appreciate them."

Already she had started. I hadn't even stepped in the door and already I could see how this day was going to go.

"You know Jayden can give you grandchildren as well, don't you? I'm not the only son here."

"Yes, I know, but he is younger and still needs to enjoy life."

"I think he has enjoyed life enough for ten people and needs to settle down as much as I do," I said with a smile on my face.

"Thanks, bro. Don't think Mum needs to know that," Jayden said, as he walked over to me and gave me a hug.

"Oh, I think she does, Jayden. Like that time…."

"Yeah, that's enough of that." Jayden cut me off as I started to laugh.

"At least one of my boys is good, aren't you Monty? Come on, let's see what treats I have for you, boy," Mum said, calling Monty into the house.

"He will get fat if you keep giving him treats," I said, raising my eyebrows at her.

"Nonsense, he's a growing boy," she replied, as she walked through the front door.

Stepping in the front door after my brother, I saw my Dad standing there waiting for us.

"Hey, Dad. How are you?" I asked, walking up to him to give him a hug.

"I'm doing good. Thanks, Mason, and you? How's business?" he asked.

"Yeah, it's good, just got a corporate client, which makes a change from the lying and cheating partners we usually have to deal with."

"You can say that again, bro." Jayden added.

"Coffee?" Dad asked.

"Silly question, Dad. When have you known me to turn down a coffee?" I asked, following him into the kitchen.

Sitting down at the table in the centre of the kitchen, I watched my Dad making coffee. As usual Jayden went and spent time with Mum, and I tended to spend most of my time with Dad.

"So, now that it's just the two of us, how are you really getting on, Mason?" my dad asked.

"I've been worse, but I did want to talk to you about something. Can we go out for our usual walk later? I know Jayden won't want to join us."

"OK, son. We do have our best chats on a walk, don't we? We'll go out after lunch." He passed me my coffee.

Walking into the living room with Dad, I found Mum and Jayden in their usual spot on the settee, with Monty snuggled up to Mum on her lap. Smiling, I realised that the fact I could never get him off the furniture was thanks to mum. She treated my dog like a child at times. Really, though, I didn't care. He was almost like a child to me, as well as my best friend and companion. I wouldn't tell Brandon that, though.

We sat in the room just chatting about nothing in particular. Mum went on about their trip to Rome, somewhere they had both wanted to go for years, and now they had the money and time to, they could go wherever they wanted. She told us about the colosseum and their trip to the Vatican and how they had seen the Pope give an address to the people of Rome. It sounded like a fantastic trip, and I decided that if I ever got the chance I would take Jess with me.

There she was again, slipping into my thoughts. I hadn't even asked her out and I was already planning romantic holidays to Rome. Really, I needed to get a grip on myself, and I was hoping my chat with Dad would do the trick. He hadn't dated much, in fact the only real dates he had been on was with my Mum. They had been together since they were sixteen, nearly thirty-four years together now, but he understood what I was going through all the same.

We all sat down as usual at 1:00 for lunch, a roast as always. Mum's roasts were the best, but then I probably was quite biased when it came to my Mum. She would always make sure Jayden and I had a proper dinner on a Sunday if we were there. I'm sure she thought we didn't eat for the rest of the week.

We sat there eating and discussing nothing in particular. Mum would often slip in something about me finding myself a good girl to settle down with and have kids. As usual, I would just brush her off, saying that I am sure I would find someone and give her as many grandchildren as she wanted, much to my brother's amusement.

Sitting there after we had helped Mum clear away all the lunch plates and pots and pans, Dad got up and suggested we go for a walk. As usual he invited Mum and Jayden, but as normal they both declined. It was as if we all knew what we needed, Jayden and Mum time, and Dad and me time.

Standing up, I gave my Mum a quick kiss on the cheek and said that I would see her in a little while. Then I went to put on my coat and grabbed Monty's lead just in case I needed it. Calling Monty over, Dad and I walked out of the front door and started our walk in the surrounding countryside of my parents' house.

We hadn't been walking more than a couple of minutes when my Dad started to speak.

"So, what has got you all worked up that you need to have a chat then, son? I know it's not your mother going on about finding yourself a nice girlfriend," he said.

"Well, it is, and it isn't," I replied. "I have met someone, but I'm not sure if she likes me. And even if she does, I really don't know how to go about asking her," I continued.

"Oh, I see. Tell me about her."

"Well, she owns the local coffee shop in the town."

"Oh, Jessica, you mean."

"You know her?"

"Not really, I just know that the coffee shop in Kings View is called Jessica's Coffee House, so I assumed that was her name. Mum and I have met her a couple of times when we have been down to visit. She seems like a lovely young lady and a fellow business person. I am sure you would be perfect for each other."

"But, how can you be so sure? We hardly know each other. Up until five days ago we hadn't even spoken. How can I know the feelings I have aren't just lust resulting from not being with a woman for over three years? How can I be sure she is the right one for me, Dad?"

"You already know that she is. You just told me so."

"What do you mean?"

"You have feelings for her. You obviously can't get her out of your mind, because I knew something was bothering you as soon as you walked through the door today."

"You're right about not being able to get her out of my mind, that's for sure. I'm not going to tell you what happened in the shower this morning," I said, as a quick chuckle left my lips.

"No, I don't think I want to know. There are still some things that parents and their kids shouldn't share," he said with a laugh.

"What should I do about it though, Dad? I never had a problem asking a girl out before Cassandra, but she ruined everything for me. Now I just don't know if I can put my love and trust into anyone again."

"Just talk to her Mason. Ask her if she would like to get to know you better. Just start off as friends and then go from there. If it's meant to be, it's meant to be. If not, then at least you know you tried. Do not let her slip away from you because you were too scared to try," he said, as he put his hand on my shoulder.

"Thanks, Dad. You always give the best advice."

"Anytime, son, and don't worry. I won't mention this to mum until you are sure, and then I will let you have the honours. However, just remember as soon as you mention a girlfriend, she will probably start planning the wedding and turning one of the spare bedrooms into a nursery," he said with glee in his voice.

"I know. That's what I am worried about."

We headed back to the house in silence, my mind going around in circles with what to do about Jess. Walking back, I decided I needed some space to think away from everyone. When we arrived, I decided to make an excuse about having some work to do so I could get off home. Saying goodbye to my parents and brother, I got Monty into the car and started on my drive. There were a lot of things I had to go through in my head, including how I was going to make Jess mine.

Chapter Ten

Jessica

I t was just after 1:00 on Sunday afternoon, and the shop had been open for three hours. Maddie was in her usual spot at the window watching the world go by, and the morning rush had finished. Being Sunday, I had soon realised that most people didn't turn up until just after 10:00, enjoying a lie in. I quickly decided that I wouldn't open until 10:.00 and would close around 4:00 p.m., giving me both a lie in and time to get things ready for the following week.

Making a latte for Maddie and a hot chocolate for me, I picked them up and joined Maddie for a chat. If any customers came in then I could go and serve them, but it was highly unlikely now. I was starting to wonder whether it was worth continuing to open in the afternoon, but turning customers away was not my style.

"How's everything with you, Maddie?" I placed the latte in front of her and took a sip from my hot chocolate.

"Thanks, Jess. I'm good, busy with college work. I only have one more term before my final exams and then I suppose I will have to go and get a real job. Problem is, there aren't many jobs going for someone with a psychology degree here in Kings View."

"Well, you always have a job here until you get yourself sorted. The customers love you and I know you could do with the money. Anyway, you should speak to Jayden and Tyler. I'm sure your skills could be used by them, even if it is just on a consultation basis."

"That's true. I hadn't thought of that and you could always put in a good word with Mason," she replied, lifting her eyebrows.

"Yeah, I'm sure my word is going to get you a job, Maddie. We have hardly spoken; why he would listen to me I don't even know."

"As I keep saying to you, you just keep telling yourself that he is not interested and you might just convince me. Mason is very into you. You can see it every time he looks at you with those eyes. The problem is, neither of you knows how to break the ice."

Sitting there for a moment, hugging my hot chocolate in my hands, I considered what Maddie had said. Was she right? Did Mason and I just not know how to break the ice? Or was it just that we didn't want a relationship? I wondered if something happened in Mason's past, as I was sure a guy like him would have women falling at his feet. Maybe not here in Kings View as the average age here was over fifty, but still, he could go and find any woman he wanted if he tried. As I sat there pondering, I was pulled from my thoughts by the shop bell ringing.

Looking up, I saw Chris had walked in, so I got up from the table and walked to the counter to serve him.

"Hi Chris, we don't usually see you on a Sunday. What can I do for you?"

"Hi, Jess. My job finished early, so I was hoping to get something for lunch. Do you have any soup left?"

"Yeah, I do. It's tomato and red pepper today. Will that be OK for you?"

"That would be fab, thanks."

"Do you want it to take away?"

"If you don't mind, that would be great, and a roll to go with it as well," he called after me as I went to the back to get it ready.

I gathered his meal and returned to the counter.

"Anything to drink?" I asked, placing his food on the counter.

"You know I can't resist your Hazelnut lattes."

"OK, coming right up," I said, stepping to the coffee machine to start making it for him.

Placing his drink in front of him, I took the money he gave me and handed him his change.

"Thanks, babe. I'll see you in the morning as usual."

"You're welcome. See you in the morning."

With that, he took his food and drink and walked out of the shop.

"Babe? Since when does Chris call you babe?" Maddie asked, as I walked back over to her table and sat down.

"I know, it's quite unsettling actually. He started calling me babe on Monday morning. I thought he was just being friendly, but to me his tone doesn't suggest it."

"That's just weird and slightly worrying, Jess. With everything else that is going on, you need to be careful with Chris. You know what I went through for those few months."

"I know. I will have a word with him, but I don't want to upset him. He has been a really good friend to me. I'm sure he's just using it as a term of endearment and doesn't mean anything by it."

"Well, just be careful."

"I will."

"Anyway, speaking of everything that is going on, how are things with your situation? Any more strange occurrences in your flat?"

"Not since the knives went missing. The police aren't worried about it, even with knives vanishing. The officer I spoke to suggested I should get a priest in to remove the poltergeist I obviously had."

"You have got to be kidding me, poltergeist, really?"

"I know, right? They just think it's a laugh, and until I am attacked or even killed there is nothing they can do about it."

"Jess, I think you should go and see Mason and explain everything to him. He is a private investigator after all. He may be able to help or know someone that can at least. I don't like you being in that flat alone. I can come and stay with you if you would like."

"That's very sweet of you, Maddie, but I'm sure I will be fine. As the police said, nothing has happened to me. I just worry that someone is getting into my flat somehow. It's probably just me going mad, and I've moved stuff around in my sleep or something. There is something else, though."

"What's that?"

"Have you noticed a strange guy standing across the road and a black truck driving past?"

"Can't say I have, but then my head has been in my laptop all week, so I hardly pay any attention to what's going on around me. Why?"

"Nothing really. It might just be that I am so on edge. It's just I have noticed this guy, dressed all in black with a hat and sunglasses on. He just stands over the other side of the road and stares at the shop. Then there is this black truck that keeps driving past."

"Jess, please take this seriously. I couldn't stand to see you get hurt."

"I will, Maddie. But it's probably just nothing."

"I must be on my way. I have an assignment due tomorrow. Are you going to be OK here on your own?"

"I will be fine. You get going. I might need you to look after the shop for a while tomorrow, though. I might go and chat with Mason in the morning, but only if it's OK with you."

"Of course I will. It would make me happier if you did anyway."

"Thanks, honey. See you tomorrow".

"See you tomorrow, Jess."

With that, Maddie left the shop and I was alone. I looked up at the clock, just a little after 3 p.m. It was time to get myself into gear and ready for tomorrow. Walking to the back, I checked to see how much soup I had left, and there was just enough for me to have dinner tonight unless anyone came in and wanted some. Deciding to leave it there for the time being, I cleaned down all the surfaces and took a couple of batches of croissants and rolls out of the freezer, ready to cook tomorrow morning.

There was no way I was making any today. I had enough for Tuesday as well, if I didn't get a chance to make any tomorrow, and I would deal with that Tuesday afternoon if I needed to. I checked that I had a couple of pastries left over for Chris in the morning and put them in a bag.

Deciding I would get the soup for tomorrow ready upstairs in my kitchen and then bring it down later, I took out the last serving from the slow cooker for me to have for dinner tonight and washed up the slow cooker pot. Placing my soup and roll into the empty pot, I walked out into the shop to make sure everything was clean and tidy for the morning.

Walking up to the shop door, I turned the sign to closed, seeing there was no one in the street outside and locked the door. It was only just before 4 p.m., so I wasn't closing too early. I turned off the shop lights, and walked to the back and gathered all my bits and pieces to make soup for tomorrow and my dinner for the night, and locked up the shop to head up to my flat.

This was the part I had started to dread every day. What I was going to find when I walked into my flat in the evening? Was there anything that was going to be missing or would something turn back up? Opening up my front door, I stepped into my flat, the feeling of dread immediately radiating through me. All seemed in place as I scanned the front room. All my photos were still in position and nothing appeared to be missing.

I walked into the kitchen and placed everything down on the table in the middle of the room and looked around. Again, nothing seemed out of place. Maybe I really was going mad. The stuff I thought was missing must be in the flat somewhere. Walking into my bedroom, again seeing that nothing was out of place, I decided to change into a pair of leggings and a baggy jumper just so I could relax a bit.

Placing my jeans in the washing basket, I noticed that my pjs I had placed in there this morning were not on the top of the pile. Someone had gone through my dirty washing. OK, this was starting to get extremely weird. Why would someone go through my dirty washing? Was I going mad?

I walked back into the kitchen and started to make myself a coffee and sat down at the table. I must have been sitting there for a while just staring out into my living room, completely spaced out, when my phone chimed to let me know I had a message. I noticed that I had missed two calls from my dad, I must have zoned out big time not to have heard it.

The message read, "Hi, Jess. Just checking in to see if you are OK. Tried to call but you must be busy in the shop. Give me a call later. Dad."

Deciding that it would be best to call him first before getting involved with making the soup for tomorrow, I dialed his number.

"Hi, Jess. Sorry, I didn't mean to drag you away from whatever you were doing."

"Hi, Dad. It's not a problem. I was just carrying stuff up the stairs, so I couldn't get to my phone." OK, so that was a lie, but I didn't want to worry him with everything that was going on here.

"How are you doing? We haven't spoken to you in ages."

"I'm good, thank you, Dad. I've just been really busy with the shop. How are you and Edith?"

"Edith is good, thank you, and I am fine. We are both looking forward to popping up and seeing you next month. We have booked into Nicole's B&B, so we are all set."

"That's good. Mr. and Mrs. Duncan will be glad to hear that. They are looking forward to seeing you again. They said they haven't seen you in what seems like ages."

"I know, but we are enjoying ourselves so much down here."

"I'm glad you're happy, Dad. You deserve it, and Edith is such a lovely lady. As long as she makes you happy, that is all I ask."

"She does, but is there anyone making you happy?"

It didn't take long; I had wondered when this question would come up.

"Not yet, but I have met someone. We haven't known each other long, but I think I really like him. Problem is, I don't know if he feels the same."

"Go for it, Jess. Just speak to him. If you're feeling this way, then you can bet he is probably feeling exactly the same way. But like you, he doesn't know how to go about it. I just want to see you happy, and I haven't seen that since we lost you mother."

"I know, Dad, but it's difficult."

"Life is only as difficult as you make it, my dear. Just go with the flow and let things happen naturally, and you will find happiness."

"Thanks, Dad. You always know how to make me feel better about things."

"You're welcome, my dear. Anyway, I will let you get on, as I'm sure you're busy, but don't be a stranger, and phone me more often, please."

"I will. Love you, Dad, and send my love to Edith."

"Will do, and love you too, Jess."

With that, he hung up the phone. I spent the next hour getting the soup ready for tomorrow. Once it was all cooled, I took it down and placed it in my refrigerator in the shop, so I just had to get it out and turn it on in the morning.

Walking back into my flat, I decided I was going to take some time out for myself for a change. Maddie had been going on about this new series of books she had been reading, and I decided to find out what all the fuss was about. Pouring myself a glass of white wine, I took it into the front room, sat myself down, and opened my Kindle.

Entering Reed Security series into the search bar, I found the series of books Maddie had been talking about. *Sinner*, by Giulia Lagomarsino was the first book, so I downloaded and started to read, sipping my wine every now and then. The book was amazing, and I could see why Maddie had recommended it. I found myself inserting Mason's handsome face in the role of the hero. Before I knew it, I looked up at the clock and realised it was nearly 9 p.m., I really needed to get myself in the shower and into bed.

Closing down my Kindle, I got up from the settee and placed my empty glass into the sink, had a shower, and got ready for bed. With reading and a shower, I was feeling more relaxed about my situation. Getting into bed, I covered myself up, and as soon as my head hit the pillow I fell into a deep sleep.

Chapter Eleven

Jessica

The alarm blaring next to me shook me from my sleep, 4:30 a.m. already, and time to start a new day. Last night was one of the best night's sleep I had in the last week, and I must have been more tired than I realised.

Getting out of bed, I was excited for once to start the day. Today was the day I was going to start putting everything behind me and I was going to go to King Investigations to try and sort out all of the strange happenings in my flat.

Stepping into my bathroom, I went through my normal morning routine, making sure to add a little extra makeup as I knew I was going to be seeing Mason later, and then got dressed for the day. Coffee was next on the agenda, and I walked into the kitchen to start making a cup. Starting the coffee machine and placing a mug onto the counter ready, I walked out into my living room and stopped dead in my tracks.

There on the coffee table was a smashed picture frame. Looking up at my mantelpiece, I noticed the picture of Sean and me was missing. Walking over to the table, I found the picture was lying on it but Sean had been torn off it, just leaving a picture of me. Next to it was a typed note that just said:

Roses are Red
Violets are Blue
He took from Me
So I'll Take YOU!

I was frozen and just stared down at the note trying to understand what it meant. What did my brother take and from who? It didn't make any sense. Suddenly I felt sick, rushing into the bathroom, tears pouring down my face. I collapsed on the floor dry heaving into the toilet. What the hell was going on? I hadn't done anything to deserve any of this and I was sure my brother Sean hadn't either.

Sitting on the floor for a while, tears falling down my face, I finally managed to pull myself up and look at myself in the mirror. So much for trying to make myself look good for Mason. I was a mess. Brushing my teeth and fixing my face for a second time I was starting to look human again. Stepping out into the corridor, I walked back into my kitchen and finished making my coffee.

Walking out with the coffee in my hand, I sat down on the settee and looked at the destroyed photo and note on the table. Now I had a good reason to go to King's, along with the police. This was the threat they needed to be able to do something, but I didn't want to be laughed at again, so King's it was.

Deciding to leave the note there, I had watched enough tv investigation and forensic shows to know that you shouldn't touch any evidence. I thought it best to get out of the flat and make myself busy, at least that way I might be able to forget it for a while before I had to explain it all to someone. I grabbed my phone to take a picture, just in case the note disappeared before anyone got here to read it. Laughing to myself, I was amazed at how calm I was being about this. It must be shock, that's it, I am in shock and soon everything will come crashing down on me.

How could I be this calm? Someone had been in my flat again, but this time they had threatened me. Well, I suppose saying they are going to take me isn't really a threat of harm, but still a threat. I sat at the table in silence, my mind completely blank, not knowing what to do. My phone chimed that it was 5:00 a.m., pulled me from my trance. I really had to get moving.

Everything was in the oven, and I was currently making a Hazelnut latte for Chris. It was just coming up to 5:30, and I was expecting Chris to knock on the door at any second. Chris didn't make me wait, bang on 5:30 he was at the front door knocking to get in. I double checked it was him and unlocked the door.

"Hi, Jess. You OK? You look a bit flustered."

"Hi, Chris. I'm fine, I just had a busy morning already, that's all. Your latte is on the counter, and I'll just get you your pastry."

"Thanks, Jess."

Placing the bag on the counter, I turned to Chris.

"Was there anything else?"

"No, that's everything, thank you. Are you sure you are OK?"

"Yes, just a little tired, but thanks for asking."

"OK, well if you're sure, I will let you get on. Don't forget to lock up behind me."

"Will do. See you later, Chris."

Chris walked out of the shop, and I locked the door behind him.

It was a typical Monday morning. Mr. Duncan came in at 6.30 and placed his typical lunch order, and the usual customers came and went on their way to work. Maddie arrived at around

8.30, and I managed to explain everything that had happened this morning in between serving customers.

"Jess, you really need to do something about this now. That is a serious threat."

"I know. It has really freaked me out this morning. Would you mind looking after the shop while I go to King's and speak to Mason. At least he won't laugh at me and tell me it's a ghost. Well, at least I hope he won't."

"Of course I will, Jess. I definitely think it's for the best."

"I was hoping one of the guys would pop in this morning so I could give them a warning I was going to stop by."

As the words left my mouth Jayden and Tyler walked through the door.

"The usual, Jayden?"

"Yes, please."

"Actually, I am glad you popped in. I wanted to have a quick chat. I was hoping I could stop into your offices a bit later and perhaps have a chat with Mason. A couple of strange things have happened in my flat and was hoping you would all be able to help."

"Not a problem. Why don't you pop in around 11.00? You could bring our lunch order with you to save us coming round."

"OK, thank you. I really appreciate it."

"Not a problem. Anytime, and I'm sure Mace will be pleased to see you."

He passed me the money for the coffees and lunch order, and Maddie handed over the coffees that she had been making while I was talking to Jayden. Tyler took two of the coffees from Maddie.

"Thanks, Maddie," he said with a smile.

"You're welcome, Tyler," she replied, starting to blush.

Looking at Jayden, he winked at me. I knew Tyler was about to get some stick when he walked out of the shop.

"See you both later," I said, smiling at them both as they left the shop.

Turning to Maddie, I didn't even have to say anything to her.

"What? There is nothing going on between Tyler and me, and there isn't likely to be either."

"I didn't say anything." I walked to the back to start making some of the lunch orders, so Maddie didn't have to while I was at King's.

Carrying a box full of food and drinks, I said my goodbyes to Maddie and told her to call me if she had any problems and walked out the shop to head up to King's Investigation Services. Usually, I didn't do a delivery service but, on this occasion, I would make an exception. It was only a five-minute walk, which was lucky, as this box was actually starting to get a bit heavy with five sandwiches, soups and coffees all in it.

Walking up towards the office building, I noticed Jayden just walking inside with Monty in tow.

"Trying to get yourself a woman, are you Jayden?"

"What, all the girls pay attention to me when I have Monty with me."

"I bet they do," I said with a laugh, "but that's because you are such a good boy, isn't it Monty?"

Monty's ears immediately pricked up, and I was treated to a woof in reply.

"Don't worry, I didn't forget you, boy," I said to him, placing down the box on the front desk and passing him one of my biscuits.

"Hi, Jess." Mason's voice sounded from just around the corner as I looked up to see him standing there. Yep, he was still as gorgeous as ever.

"Hi, Mace. I hope you don't mind me giving Monty a biscuit. I couldn't come here and not bring him a treat as well. I popped some cake in the box for you all as well. My treat."

"Jess, I think I love you." Jayden went rummaging through the box.

"I am sure you say that to any woman who brings you food and cake."

"Our Mum is the only woman who brings him food, so I suppose you are right there. Anyway, before we get into a debate over that, Jayden said you wanted to have a chat. Do you want to come down to my office?"

"If that's OK, Mace. I don't want to keep you from your business."

"It's not a problem. If I can help, then it's not keeping me from anything."

Following Mason up the corridor, I walked behind him into his office and waited as he shut the door behind me.

"So, do you want to start from the beginning?" Mason asked, as he walked past me and gestured for me to sit down on the settee in his office.

I stood there for a second, not sure how to begin. Then the fear, tension, and worry that I had been experiencing for the past week built inside me and I felt myself start to shake as the tears started to fall from my eyes. My head was telling me that I couldn't show this weakness in front of Mason, that he would hate me for it, but I couldn't stop. Feeling my legs give way below me as the tears continued to fall, I braced myself to hit the ground, but I didn't.

Two strong arms engulfed my body, holding me tight against a well-toned chest. Mason was holding me, comforting me. Leaning into him, I could feel the warmth of his body radiating from him. Hearing his heart beating almost calmed me completely, and my erratic breathing started to even out as I tried to compose myself.

"It's OK, Jess. Whatever it is, we can sort it out. I can't stand to see you in this state. Come on, sit down with me and we will try and get to the bottom of whatever is going on," Mason said, still holding me tightly.

"I'm sorry, Mace. I really didn't want to break down, but this morning just took things over the edge and I really don't know what to do."

"Don't worry, we are here to help." He led me over to the settee and sat me down.

A knock at the door had Mason turning around before he sat down next to me, I was slightly relieved, as I wasn't sure I could take the closeness of his body much longer without reacting to it.

"Come in."

"Sorry to interrupt, Mace, but I thought you might want your coffee before it got cold, and I assume the hot chocolate is yours, Jess?" Jayden said as he walked through the door. Taking one look at me he continued.

"What the fuck did you do, Mace? Jess, are you OK?"

"I'm fine, Jayden. It's not Mason's fault. I just kind of lost it when I was about to tell him what was happening. I'll be fine in a second, and thanks for bringing in my drink."

"As long as you're sure? Do you want me to stay?"

"No, you're fine, thanks."

Jayden tipped his head to Mason and walked out of the door. Mason passed me my drink and sat down next to me.

"So, do you want to start at the beginning?" he asked while holding my hand in his.

I went through everything that had happened over the past week, from the missing pyjamas that reappeared the next day, the missing mug, knives, pictures and items of clothing that had all been taken. Some of those items had come back, but most were never to be seen again. Then I explained the fact that I had started to notice this creepy guy staring in the shop, and a black truck parked outside, or driving past. I also told him about the police saying I should get a priest in, as I obviously had a poltergeist living with me.

"So that was all that was happening up until this morning. I never heard anyone in the flat, except for one morning when I had a bad dream and woke immediately after hearing someone saying 'I'm coming for you,' but I really don't know if that was real or just a nightmare. Anyway, this morning I found a smashed photo frame and a picture that was of my brother and me, but he had been ripped off. Next to it was a typed note that said., 'Roses are Red, Violets are blue, He took from me, So I'll take you.' I left everything on the table at home and didn't touch anything."

Looking up at Mason, I thought he was going to scream at me with rage, he looked so angry. He took a deep breath and squeezed my hand as he looked at me and smiled.

"Sorry, I didn't mean to frighten you; I wish you had come to me sooner. I hate thinking that you have spent the last week worrying about this on your own. Do you mind if I come up to your flat to have a look?"

"Of course, I don't. I need all the help I can get. I can't afford to pay you much, but I can make sure you all get lunch every day."

"Jess, don't worry about the money, or lunch. I'll do this because I want to help you and make you feel safe."

"Thank you so much, Mace. You don't know how much that means to me."

Chapter Twelve

Mason

Sitting there listening to Jess explain everything that had happened, I could feel the anger brewing in me. No woman should feel like that in her own home or at work. Hell, no one should feel like that. I realised that the black truck Jess had mentioned must have been the same one I had seen the other day. Mrs. Duncan had also mentioned her worry about Jess and I hadn't picked up any anxiety in our conversation. My infatuation with her must have shielded me from the obvious signs. The anger must have shown on my face, because when Jess looked up at me after finishing her explanation, the fear on her face was noticeable.

"Sorry, I didn't mean to frighten you; I wish you had come to me sooner. I hate thinking that you have spent the last week worrying about this on your own. Do you mind if I come up to your flat to have a look?"

"Of course I don't. I need all the help I can get. I can't afford to pay you much, but I can make sure you all get lunch every day."

"Jess, don't worry about the money, or lunch. I'll do this because I want to help you and make you feel safe."

"Thank you so much, Mace. You don't know how much that means to me."

Smiling at her, I squeezed her hand to try and let her know she was safe. When she had broken down after walking into my office, I did the only thing I could think of, I held her. It had been the one thing I had wanted to do since I had first spoken to her, to hold her in my arms. She fit perfectly against my body, as if we were meant to be together. And when she leaned into me, her warm body against mine, I almost lifted her head to kiss her; I wanted to kiss her. However, now was not the time for that. For now, I had to try and get to the bottom of what was happening.

However, there was no way she was staying in that flat tonight on her own. Jess was either staying at my house or Monty and I would be having a sleepover. I didn't even care if I was on the sofa. Just being near her and making her feel safe was going to be my top priority now. Jess was not going to pay a penny for this. I would bear all the costs and there was no way she would change my mind.

"Do you mind if I ask the rest of the guys in here and let them know what is happening? I'm going to need their help and it would be best if you are here to answer any questions they have. If it's too much, please just say."

"No, that's fine. I would rather get this all over and sorted as quickly as possible. And Mason, thank you. I'm so glad Maddie convinced me to come to you. I thought I was going mad, especially when the police just laughed it all off."

"It's not a problem, Jess. I'm glad you came to me as well, and don't worry, I will have something to say to Detective Jenkins when I speak to him. We are old adversaries."

Walking over to my office door, I opened it and called out to

Jayden.

"Jayden, can you gather the guys together in the meeting room. I need to discuss the situation with Jess to you all."

"OK, bro, be there in five."

"Thanks, bro."

Turning to Jess, I looked down at her. Even with her puffy red eyes, she was absolutely gorgeous. She was everything in a woman I hadn't realised I needed. And god, did I need her. Walking over to her I held out my hand to help her up from the settee. A feeling of relief washed over me when she placed her hand in mine and allowed me to help her up. Pulling her towards me I hugged her again, just needing to feel her close to me to give both her and me some comfort. Jess immediately leaned into me again and I had to step away slightly before I did something we would both regret.

Lifting her head slightly to look in my eyes, I placed my hand on her cheek and spoke.

"We will get to the bottom of this Jess, I promise you."

"I know you will do everything you can, thank you."

Removing my hand from her cheek, I guided her into the meeting room to find all of the guys sitting there waiting for us to enter the room. Brandon, always the gentleman, got up from his chair and pulled one out for Jess next to mine, and I guided her to it and helped her to sit down.

"Thanks man," I said to Brandon, giving him a chin lift, firstly for the gesture, and secondly because he obviously knew Jess needed my support, so he chose the seat closest to me where he would usually sit.

Spending the next twenty minutes explaining everything to the guys, I saw the same reaction I had on their faces. The anger, the worry all showed in their eyes, and Brandon almost looked as though he was going to kill someone. We would need to have a talk about that as that was something that could not happen, well, not unless it was forced upon me.

"So, that's everything. What are your thoughts?" I said to them all.

"We need to get some surveillance cameras installed, so we can work out how they are getting in. If we're lucky, we'll also be able to see exactly who it is. I can get onto that as soon as we finish this meeting," Tyler suggested.

"Good thinking, Tyler. I suspect they will cover their tracks and we won't get a clear view of their face but it is worth a try."

"Jess, are you able to get hold of your brother and try and find out why this intruder seems to have a problem with him?" Brandon said to my right.

"I can try, however I think he is currently backpacking around Australia. He and his fiancé, Nicola wanted a holiday before their wedding later in the year."

"OK, well anything you can find out could be of help to us. Mace, are you going to go and have a look at the flat? Perhaps we can get onto our contacts at the yard and get any prints off the note, if whoever it is was silly enough to not wear gloves."

"Yeah, I was going to do that after this meeting, but I agree, the chance they left any evidence is remote. They even typed the note so we couldn't analyse the handwriting."

"There is one other thing, Mace," Jayden said looking from me to Jess.

"What's that, Jayden?"

"I really don't think Jess should stay in her flat, or if she does, then she shouldn't be alone. Whoever is doing this, they are starting to ramp up what they are doing, and the note not only proves that, but sets out a clear threat to her."

"I totally agree, but I'll speak to Jess about that once I check out her flat, if that's OK, Jess?"

"Whatever you all think. I just want to feel safe again. And after this morning, I definitely don't think I can feel safe in the flat on my own."

Relief washed through me at her words. I thought she would put up a bit more of a fight with staying in the flat on her own. However, whether she would allow me to stay there, I still had to approach.

"I just need to pop into the shop to let Maddie know what is happening."

"Not a problem. We can do that on our way up. Thanks, guys. If you think of anything else just go ahead. I trust all of you to make Jess's safety a priority, but we cannot let our other assignments get behind, so I'm afraid this might mean some overtime."

"I don't want to cause you any problems, especially for your business, Mason."

"Don't even think that. Every man in this room wants to help you and will do everything they can to make you feel safe. In fact, I'm sure they will enjoy dealing with something that isn't a cheating partner."

"Don't worry about us, Jess," Nathan replied, who had surprisingly been quiet throughout this. "We will do everything in our power to get to the bottom of this, and you will be back in your flat, safe and sound, as soon as possible."

"Thank you."

"Right, I will let you guys get on while I go and look at Jess's flat."

"You need me to come along with you?" Brandon asked, raising his eyebrows, a smirk appearing at the corner of his mouth.

Looking at him, I knew exactly what he was thinking. He had already realised that Jess meant more to me than just a damsel in distress that I was going to rescue. He knew me too well.

"No, you're fine. Thanks for the offer though, Brandon. If the perpetrator is watching, it would look too suspicious if loads of us walked into the flat. They would know Jess had gone for help. I can pass off as a friend or Jess's new boyfriend if I am on my own with her."

"Whatever you say, Mace."

With that, all the guys got up from the table and walked out of the room.

"You OK?" I asked, turning back to Jess.

"Yeah, I'm fine, just a little overwhelmed that you all want to help me."

"Why wouldn't we? We practically live at your shop for lunch every day. You are a member of the town and we want to help whoever we can. Anyway, let's get to seeing this note out of the way and get you sorted for the next few days."

Holding out my hand again, I guided her out of the office and towards her shop.

"I hope you don't mind me holding your hand. If whoever is doing this is watching, it will just look like you have brought lunch round to me and I'm now walking back with you to the shop."

"I don't mind at all. Actually, I quite like it. It's comforting."

A blush appeared on her cheeks and I smiled at her. Yes, I could most definitely get used to this. When we arrived at her shop, I opened the door for her and placed my hand on the small of her back as I guided her in. The shop was quite busy for Monday lunchtime and a young lady, who I assumed to be Maddie, was working behind the counter.

"Hi, Maddie. Sorry I have been a while, is everything OK?" Jess said to the young lady.

"Not a problem. Everything is under control. I assume this is Mason. It's good to finally meet you."

"You too, Maddie, and you can call me Mace."

"I just need to get a couple of soups ready," Maddie replied.

"OK, I'll come back with you." Jess answered her, and we both walked to the back of the shop.

"Thanks for not making things too obvious, Maddie."

"That's OK, Jess. I kind of guessed you might be pretending to be going out together in case you were being watched. Everything is good here, so please don't worry. I can stay all day if you would like. You just need to come and lock up."

"Thank you. I really appreciate it. Mace and I are just going to go upstairs to have a look around and then I'll come back down and let you know what's happening."

"OK. And thank you, Mace. I knew you would help her."

"We are going to get this all sorted. You don't need to worry about that."

With that, Maddie got two portions of soup and went out into the shop to give them to her customers.

"Shall we get this out of the way then?" I asked, giving Jess' hand a squeeze.

"Yeah, we can go out the back door, save walking back through the shop."

Jess walked to the back door and we both went through and walked up to her flat above the shop. Walking into her flat, I could see Jess visibly tense up. It was obvious she really didn't want to be in here. Walking up behind her, I placed my hand on her shoulder.

"It's OK, I'm here. Nothing is going to happen to you."

Feeling her shoulder relax slightly under my hand, I removed it, not wanting to make her feel more uncomfortable than she already was. Looking into the living room, I could see the photo and note she had told me about earlier. Walking over to it, I bent down to look more closely. Turning to look at Jess, I could see the tears starting to fall from her eyes again.

Immediately I got up and walked over to her, wrapping my arms around her into a tight hug.

"It's OK, Jess. Please don't get upset. We will get to the bottom of this, I promise."

Leaning into me, sobs escaped from her lips, and she looked up at me.

"Why is this happening to me, Mace? What have I done to deserve this, to feel like a victim in my own home?"

"I don't know, Jess, but we are going to find out. Come on, let's make you a coffee," I said, leading her out into the kitchen.

"Do you have some tongs and a couple of plastic bags? I want to put the photo and note in them so I can get them checked out by my friend at the Met police."

Jess went over to the cupboard and got out 2 plastic bags and a set of tongs from the utensil drawer.

"I'll make us both a coffee while you deal with that," she said, now the tears had finally stopped falling.

Walking out into the living room, I placed all the bits of the photo and broken frame into one bag and the note in the other, making sure not to touch them with anything other than the tongs. I left them on the coffee table and went back into the kitchen to find Jess sitting down with a coffee in front of her.

Sitting next to her, I placed the tongs down onto the table.

"Jess, I don't want you staying here tonight, for two reasons. One, I can see how upset and unsettled you were just walking in here. And two, I wouldn't be able to sleep myself knowing you were here. Would you please come and stay with me tonight? I have a three bedroom place so you could have your own room, and Monty would love to have a house guest and...."

"Mace, you can stop right there. I would love to come and stay with you. I don't think I would be able to sleep here, even if someone was staying with me. The only problem is that I would need to be back here by 5:00 tomorrow morning, so it might be a bit of an early morning wake up call for you, and I don't want to impose."

"You wouldn't be imposing, and I'm usually an early bird myself, so 5:00 a.m. is not a problem. Plus, at least we might both get some sleep if we know you are safe. Go and get some things together for a couple of days. You can stay with me as long as you need. It might also get some of the nosy parkers in the town something to talk about."

For the first time since I had met her, I finally heard Jess laugh. It filled me with warmth to hear it, to know I had done that for her, made her feel happy when everything around her was so wrong. I wanted it more, I wanted that laugh, that smile for me and me alone. Somehow, I was going to make it happen and I was going to do it soon.

Chapter Thirteen

Jessica

My body relaxed as soon as Mace mentioned staying at his house. There was no way I was going to stay here tonight. If he hadn't suggested staying at his place, I was going to speak to Maddie and ask if I could crash at hers. Instead, I got to spend the next few days with Mason in his house, and that was something I wasn't going to turn down.

Walking into my bedroom, I grabbed my small suitcase and grabbed about a week's worth of clothes. Even if I was only at Mason's for a few days, I wanted to make sure that I had enough should anything happen. Next, I walked into my bathroom to collect everything that I needed from there and placed it into my case. Zipping it up, I walked into the kitchen where I found Mason talking to someone on his phone.

"OK, I can get one of the guys to drop it off to you either later today or tomorrow morning. Not sure you are going to find anything, but it is worth a try.........OK, thanks for the help, Callum...... We'll speak soon."

"Do you have everything you need?" Mason had put down his phone and was now looking at me.

"Yes, I have enough for a week, but I can always pop up and get more if I need and it doesn't matter if I have too much. I need to go back down to the shop though, as I need to get some bits ready for tomorrow morning. That's not going to be a problem is it?"

"No, that's fine. If you leave me your front door key, then I can get Tyler in here to put up some cameras. At least then if someone turns up, we might get a lead as to who it is, but it won't intrude on your privacy since you won't be staying here."

"Whatever you think is best. I just want to feel safe and one thing I can say right now is being with you makes me feel safe."

Mason walked over to me, took one of my hands in his, and placed his other hand on my cheek. For some reason I naturally leaned my head into his hand and looked up into those gorgeous hazel eyes of his. Smiling down at me, he lowered his head, and I was sure he was going to kiss me, I wanted him to kiss me. He stopped just as he reached the top of my head and placed a soft, gentle kiss onto my forehead.

"I'm glad to hear you feel safe with me. At this time, that is all I could hope for. Come on, let's get you back down to the shop so I can get you home at a sensible time tonight."

"OK, do you mind taking my case back to your office? If I take it with me, you can guarantee I will forget it."

"Of course, I can."

Mason guided me out of the flat and locked the front door with the key I had given him. Walking down the stairs to the back of the shop, I noticed Mr. Duncan was putting some rubbish into the bins at the back of his shop.

"Afternoon, Mr. Duncan. Sorry I wasn't there for your lunch order today."

"That's perfectly fine, Jess, my dear. Maddie explained you needed to sort a few things out. Mason, good to see you. Take care of her, please, or you will have to answer to Mabel Duncan, and believe me, that is a scary thought."

"I will look after her, Mr. Duncan. You don't have to worry about that."

"Good to hear, Mason. Are you going somewhere, Jess?"

"I am going to stay with Mason for a couple of days, Mr. Duncan. I just had a couple of things happen and Mason is going to sort them out for me. You might see Tyler or Jayden at my flat. If you do, don't worry."

"I do worry about you. You've looked really tired lately. Mason, make sure she gets a proper meal and a good night's sleep."

"I will make sure of it, Mr. Duncan."

"You make sure she does. Will you be open in the morning, Jess? If not, please don't worry."

"I will make sure I'm here for your order at 6:30. No need for you or Mrs. Duncan to worry."

"OK, well don't worry if things change and you aren't there. We will have our usual lunch order, though."

"See you in the morning, Mr. Duncan."

Walking back into the shop, I saw that there were only two customers left from the lunch rush and Maddie had started getting everything ready for the morning.

"Sorry I was a while, Maddie. I had to pack a case. I'm going to stay with Mason for a few days."

"I think that's a good idea. You might finally get a good night's sleep."

"Has it really been keeping you awake?"

"Only since waking up from the nightmare."

"I'm telling you that wasn't a nightmare. He was in your room, Jess. You said it yourself, that you could feel him breathing."

Mason chimed in, "We'll speak about this later, Jess! I'm going back to the office, and I'll pick you up about 5:00 p.m."

Mason leaned over and gave me a kiss on the cheek.

"See you later, Maddie, and thanks for helping Jess out today."

"Anytime, Mace."

With that, Mason left my shop with my case in tow. Still shocked at the kiss, I realised that I hadn't even said goodbye to him. Looking over at Maddie, I could see the big grin on her face. She was loving every minute of this.

"Something amusing you?"

"Absolutely nothing. Well, OK, that is a bit of a lie. The look of shock on your face when Mason kissed you was a picture. I think that's why he didn't worry about you not saying goodbye to him."

"I can't believe I didn't say goodbye. Do you think he will forgive me?"

"I think you can make it up to him a bit later, if you catch my drift." She served up an obnoxious wink.

"I'm going to go finish getting everything ready for the morning. Can you make me a mocha, please?"

"Nice deflection. One mocha on its way."

Walking back into the kitchen, I took in how much Maddie had done. She had basically gotten everything ready for the next day; there was nothing left for me to do. Three trays of pastries were out on the side, with three more in the cooler. I could see twelve trays of rolls in the proofing oven, all ready for baking in the morning.

Plus, it looked as though we were having oxtail soup for lunch tomorrow. I wasn't even going to ask where she managed to get the oxtail from and where she found the recipe. It was lucky she had thought of it though, as I had no idea what soup I was going to make. It would have probably ended up as vegetable again.

Tidying up everything in the back, I walked through into the shop and sat down next to Maddie at her usual table.

"Seriously, Maddie, I cannot thank you enough. I don't know what I would have done without you today, or the past week, come to think of it."

"Jess, it has really been a pleasure. Honestly, I have enjoyed today and I might take you up on your offer of helping out here. I can now see how busy it gets."

"Maddie, you are welcome to a job here whenever and however long you want it. Even if it is just a stop gap until you can find yourself a real job. As I said, I wouldn't have gotten through the past week without you."

"Thank you, Jess. I really appreciate it. Anyway, let's change the subject and get onto the topic of conversation I'm dying to ask you about. What's the deal between you and Mason?"

"There is no deal. He offered me a place to stay while we were sorting out everything that's been happening and he thought it would be a good idea to pretend we were going out together. That's it."

"That kiss was not a 'pretend we are going out together' kiss, Jess. He really meant that, and believe me, I would know."

"Stop trying to make something out of nothing, Maddie. Mason is just a caring guy who is looking out for me. I don't think he is interested in any kind of relationship. I kind of get the impression he has been seriously hurt in the past, and that's why he hasn't got a girlfriend."

"Jess, had you ever thought that you have been thrown together to save each other? He is there to help you from this weird stalker and perhaps you are there to mend his broken heart? Don't let the chance pass you by; you could both be happy for once."

Sitting there sipping my mocha, I considered everything that Maddie had just said. It was basically the same advice that my Dad had given me last night. Don't let him get away without at least trying. Were they both right? Was this an opportunity to finally find someone who wanted me for me and not someone who just wanted a quick shag when they were bored like all my last boyfriends? Maddie pulled me back from my thoughts.

"I better get off. I need to get some work done on my final dissertation. There are only a few weeks to go now."

"I'm sorry. I've kept you from your college work today."

"It's not a problem. As I said, I've enjoyed it. Anytime you need some help just give me a shout."

She got up from the table and placed her mug into the dishwasher, along with the plates and mugs the customers had left since leaving the shop a while ago. Walking up to me, she gave me a big hug, one that I really needed right then.

"I'll let you get on, it's nearly 5:00 and Mason will be here soon. I will see you at my normal time and place in the morning. Try to get a good night's rest."

"I will, and thank you again for today."

"Anytime, hun."

With that, she walked out of the shop. I spent the next 20 minutes tidying everything in the shop and getting ready for the next day. I looked up at the clock and noticed it was nearly 5:00. Making sure everything was done in the back, I locked the back door from the inside so we could leave from the front when the shop closed. There were never many customers after 5:00 p.m. on a Monday, so I decided that as soon as Mason arrived we would head off. After the morning I had, I could use a nice relaxing evening.

Maddie had everything ready for tomorrow, so there wasn't much for me to do. Hearing the bell on the shop door ring, I looked up to see Mason standing there, looking as gorgeous as ever. In that brief second I decided to throw caution to the wind and take everyone's advice. I was going to see where whatever this thing was between us could go.

"Hey, good day in the office?"

"Apart from spending the day worrying about you, yes, it was good."

"You don't have to worry about me. I'm a big girl, and I can take care of most things."

"I still worry about you. I don't like you being here, especially on your own like this. What time do you usually close? I left Monty at the office, as I didn't want to bring him round if you weren't closing for a while."

"I usually close the shop sometime between 5:00 and 6:00 p.m. It's always quiet on a Monday afternoon, and I'm all finished here thanks to Maddie, so we can head off now if you would like."

A smile appeared on his face, and I didn't think he could look any more gorgeous, but in that one second he did. His hazel eyes lit up with delight and it was a sight I wanted to see more. Was it my imagination, or did I see those beautiful eyes looking down at me like I was his world and he couldn't live without me?

"Come on, let's get out of here. The shopping I ordered should be delivered at about six, so I can cook us a meal tonight. How does salmon sound?"

"It sounds absolutely perfect. Let me grab my bag and we can lock up here."

I grabbed my bag and keys and walked out the front to where Mason was still standing. Taking the hand he was holding out for me, I allowed him to guide me out of the shop, turning off the lights on the way, and out onto the street. Locking the shop door, we walked together hand in hand up to his office and stopped next to his 4x4.

"I'll just go in and get Monty, if you want to get yourself comfortable. See you in a sec."

He lifted my hand to his lips and placed a kiss on it. I felt tingles go down the whole of my arm. Yes, I could get used to this. Letting my hand go, he gave me a smile and walked into the office to get Monty.

Chapter Fourteen

Mason

I'll just go in and get Monty, if you want to get yourself comfortable. See you in a sec."

Lifting her hand to my lips, I placed a kiss on it. Seeing the reaction on her face was all I wanted at that moment. It was obvious it affected her, her cheeks turned a slight pink where she was blushing was the exact reaction I had wanted. This could go somewhere. She did feel the same way as me, and I could feel it. All the times today I had held her, the way she moved into me, we fit together perfectly.

When I had gone back to the office earlier, Brandon had come into my office. He had made some excuse about wanting to talk about a job, but I knew it was just a front. He really wanted to know about Jess and me. He had seen it earlier when we were in the meeting room and he made it plainly obvious then he knew.

The rest of the guys seemed oblivious to it, including my brother, but Brandon knew me, really knew me. He wouldn't let this go easily, not after everything we had been through together after Cassandra.

To my surprise, he hadn't told me to be cautious, in fact, the opposite. He had said the chemistry between Jess and I was obvious, and that I would be a fool to ignore it. OK, we all remember the quote from Speed where Keanu Reeves turns to Sandra Bullock and says, "I have to warn you, I've heard relationships based on intense experiences never work." But it was a chance I wanted to take, and as Sandra said, "we can always base it on sex."

Smiling to myself, I walked into Jayden's office where Monty was currently sitting next to Jayden, being spoiled rotten as usual.

"He won't want any dinner if you keep giving him treats like that."

"He's a sprocker; of course he will still want his dinner. Jess finished for the day?"

"Yeah, she's waiting out in the car. I just came in to get Monty and then we're going to head off. Can you lock up here?"

"Sure thing, bro. Tyler's going to head over to her flat in a while and put up a few cameras. If anyone sees him he's just going to say she has an electrical problem and is staying with her boyfriend. That should get a few tongues wagging. Talking of boyfriends, are you going to admit to me that Jess is more than just a damsel in distress you want to rescue?"

"Don't know what you are talking about."

"Come on, Mace. Don't give me that. I saw the way you were both looking at each other earlier; do not tell me you're not going to give things a go between you. You're perfect for each other."

"We'll see how things go. I don't want to push her into anything.

She has a hell of a lot going on in her life right now, and I don't want to complicate matters."

"Just don't let her get away, please. Even with everything that's going on, this is the happiest I've seen you in a long time. You hardly ever leave this office before 7:00, and here you are trying to get out the door by 5:00. Just give it a chance."

"Who's the older brother here? It's meant to be me giving relationship advice to you, not the other way around."

"Whatever, bro. Go on, get out of here to the fantastic women out there waiting for you. I'll see you in the morning. The guys and I are going to base ourselves here while we're trying to sort out this situation with Jess."

"Thanks, Jayden. I appreciate it. See you in the morning. Come on boy, let's get home."

Walking out of the office with Monty in tow, I stepped outside and put him into the back of the car before getting into the driver's seat next to Jess.

"Sorry about the wait. I had to have a chat with Jayden. Tyler's going to pop into your flat later to set up some cameras; hopefully we might get some footage that will help us."

"Not a problem, and thank you again. You and the guys have been so kind and helpful. I really don't know what I would have done today without you all."

"Stop thanking me, Jess. I'm happy to help. Come on, let's get some food inside us, and then perhaps we can relax for a bit. Or we can go for a walk with Monty if you feel up to it?"

"That would be great. I love a good walk in the country."

"Let's get going then."

Starting the car, I drove off towards my house. It was strange to have someone sitting next to me, but I liked it. The thought of going home and having someone there to talk with, to spend time with, was a dream I had for a long time, but something I didn't think I would have after Cassandra. Driving along, we both sat in silence, not really knowing what to say to each other. But it didn't feel uncomfortable, at least not to me. Finally, I decided to break the silence.

"Not too far to go now. I only live about fifteen minutes from town."

"That's fine. It's a beautiful drive. You're so lucky to live in the countryside. I wish I could, but cost and necessity dictates my flat."

"I can understand that. I bought this place when we relocated down here. I love the country and wouldn't want to live anywhere else now."

"Why did you decide to relocate from the city to a dead end town like this?"

"Now, that's a long story and probably one to chat over dinner."

"Sorry, I didn't mean to intrude. You don't have to tell me."

"It's fine. It's not one of my happiest times, but I don't mind talking about it, not now, anyway. Here we go, home sweet home," I said as I pulled into the driveway.

"It's beautiful, Mason, and so secluded."

"It does me and Monty well. And I can have someone stay if they want. Mum and Dad sometimes come down, but as they only live thirty minutes away, they hardly stay now. Brandon and Jayden sometimes stay the night if they have a late night in the office and don't want to travel back home, but most of the time it's just me and Monty. Come on, let's get you settled."

Getting out of the car, I quickly walked around to Jess's door and managed to get it open before she opened it herself. Helping her out of the car, we stood almost touching. Looking down at her,

I just wanted to kiss her, to feel her soft lips against mine. We both stood there, neither of us trying to move, just gazing into each other's eyes, until a bark from the back of the car caught our attention. We both looked around and Jessica started to laugh.

"Way to break the mood, Monty," she said turning back to me, a smile lighting up her face.

"I think someone wants his dinner. Come on, let's get him sorted before I have a riot on my hands."

Taking her hand, I closed the car door and led her to the back of the car to get Monty out. We walked together up to the house and I opened the door to let her inside.

"I'll get your case in a second. Let me just sort Monty out first."

Jess followed me into the kitchen, and while I sorted out Monty's food, she started to make a coffee.

"You're not at work now, you know."

"I know, but if I'm going to be staying here, I can make myself useful, and I know you don't survive well without caffeine," she said smiling.

"I really am going to have to have words with my staff about my so-called coffee addiction."

Placing Monty's bowl down, I went back out to the car to get Jess's case and brought it back into the house.

"I will just leave this here for the moment; I'll let you choose which room you want to stay in."

As I said that, I nearly added that she could always sleep in mine, but managed to hold myself back before I ruined any chance I may have going out with her.

"Thanks again, Mace. I am sure either room will be fine. Here, I made you a latte."

"Thank you," I said, as I walked over to the table in the kitchen.

"I usually take Monty out for a walk before I have dinner, but we can have dinner first if you would prefer to get to bed early?"

"I don't want to upset Monty's routine. I know how irritable they can get if you change things. Mum and Dad used to have a spaniel when I was younger, so I know how grumpy they can get."

"OK, I'm just going to get out of this suit. Do you need to get changed?"

"No, I am fine like this."

"OK, be back in a few minutes."

Walking into my bedroom, I quickly got changed into a pair of jeans and a t-shirt. Chucking on a hoodie, I went to walk back in the kitchen. Jess stood there, gazing out the window, the evening sun shining through onto her face and hair. God, I was going to be spending most of my time in a cold shower before this week was up.

"You ready?"

A gasp escaped Jess' mouth as she jumped, startled by me.

"Sorry, I didn't mean to startle you."

"It's OK, I'm just not used to having someone else around, I guess. It might just take me a little while to get used to."

"You and me both, I suspect. Are you ready for a walk?"

"Yes, let's get Monty out."

Walking over to the door with Jess just behind me, I found Monty in his usual spot waiting to go out the door. Picking up his lead, just in case it was needed, I opened the door and let him run out. Turning to Jess, I held out my hand and again she placed hers into mine. Closing the door behind us, I lead her out into the countryside.

We walked together, side by side for a while, not saying anything, just comfortable together. Monty would run off for a while, and then run back as usual, just to make sure that we were still around.

"You are so lucky having this right on your doorstep, being able to just get out into nature and not have any care in the world."

"That was one of the reasons I chose the cottage. That, and the fact that I could finally have a dog. A London Penthouse doesn't really lend itself to a four legged pet."

"You gave up a London Penthouse for this?"

"You wouldn't have?"

Of course I would have, but then again, I probably wouldn't have chosen a London flat in the first place. It's far too busy for me. I like the peace and quiet of Kings View."

"That was another reason why I chose this cottage. It was close to a town to continue our business, and close enough to London where most of our business comes from. I just couldn't stay there myself anymore."

"Do you want to talk about it?"

"Although it's a long story, there really isn't much to tell. I was engaged to a beautiful woman called Cassandra. Well, she was beautiful when I met her, then I learned the true meaning to beauty being only skin deep. It's very difficult holding up a relationship when you're in the forces, especially when you're Special Forces. I spent a great deal of my time fighting Afghan rebels and Al-Qaeda on my tours. The things I saw. Well let's put it this way, they leave a mark on a man. One that makes it difficult to live a normal life." She glanced over at me with a look of admiration.

"I could be deployed at a moment's notice to god knows where in the world. Whenever I came home, I felt as though Cassandra was growing more distant with me. I had my suspicions that she had been seeing other men but she always denied it." I looked to Jess to catch her reaction, but she just listened and continued walking.

"When I came out of the forces, I set up the business with Brandon to start off with, and Jayden and the other guys were going to come along later once they had finished their tours. Business was good, and we were making good money. I rented a place for Cassandra to live, gave her a credit card, all the things a loving fiancé would do." I thought this next part would be hard to talk about, but I just felt a sense of relief, as if speaking to Jess about it was therapeutic.

Then I finally found out the truth. She had been having an affair with a married man. Brandon unfortunately was the one that had to witness everything and take the pictures as it was actually a job we had been given by the wife. I am sure he wasn't the first. She tried to deny it all but that was it for me; I stopped paying her rent and cancelled all of her credit cards. I moved out of London a few months after that. I don't know what happened to her and I don't really care. So there you go, that's my tale of woe."

"I'm sorry you had to go through that." Her tone was sincere, but I didn't sense pity, which made me feel grateful.

"It's OK, it's all in the past now."

"It's not though, is it? That is why you are probably considered to be Kings View's most eligible bachelor."

"I don't know if I would go that far, but probably, yes. Up until recently, I didn't think I would be able to have any feelings for another woman for as long as I lived. That is also why I'm probably considered to be a recluse up here in the downs."

"I wouldn't say a recluse, just mysterious, and why do you say up until recently?"

We both stopped for a second and I turned to look at her. Jess was standing there looking up at me with her gorgeous amber eyes. It had been the first time I had noticed how unusual her eyes were. We both just stood there, gazing at each other. Placing my hand on her cheek, I barely got out the words, "I said it because until recently, I hadn't met you."

Letting the words sink in for a moment, I put my arm around her and pulled her into my body, loving the feeling of her next to me. Hoping I was doing the right thing and not about to make a complete fool of myself, I slowly moved my head towards hers. It seemed like an eternity, but in reality it was only a few seconds before our lips touched.

It was so much better than I had imagined yesterday in the shower. Her lips were so soft. As a small breath passed her lips, I took the opportunity to run my tongue over her bottom lip and to my relief she opened, allowing me to kiss her deeply. I felt one of her arms come around me while the other went into my hair, pulling me in closer to her. Moving my hand into her hair, we kissed like it was the only thing keeping us both alive. Yes, I needed Jess in my life, I needed her in my house and in my bed, and I hoped that she wanted it too.

Chapter Fifteen

Jessica

⸻ ❧ ⸻

Standing there in beautiful surroundings, I couldn't quite believe what was happening to me. Mason King, the most gorgeous man in Kings View, was currently kissing me like his life depended on it. After everything that had happened to me, this was the last thing I had been expecting. I hoped it would happen, but I never thought it would.

We both seemed to pull away at exactly the same time, needing to take a breath, the lust in Mason's eyes was clear to see.

"I'm s......"

"Don't you dare say you're sorry for doing that Mason, please. I don't think I could take that kind of rejection right now."

"I was going to say, I'm so sorry that I waited that long to kiss you, that I wished I had done it sooner. That perhaps if I had met you earlier, you wouldn't have gone through everything this week. But hell no, I'm not rejecting you, if anything, it has just made me realise that I want you more."

He pulled me back into his body and I allowed my head to rest on his shoulder. I wasn't short by any means. At five feet, seven inches I was actually quite tall, and always had an issue finding men taller than me. However, at over six feet, I had found just that in Mason. Relaxing in his arms, feeling his warmth radiating through me, I felt at ease, like I had finally come home, hoping this wasn't just Mason feeling sorry and protective of me.

A pair of paws bounding into us and a short bark announced Monty's presence next to us. Thank god he hadn't run off. I felt Mason's chest vibrate with laughter and looked up to see the most gorgeous smile on his face.

"Way to spoil the mood again, Monty. You're starting to make a habit of this."

He let me go, and I immediately missed his body next to mine.

"Come on, let's get Monty walked, then we can grab some dinner and relax."

"I'd like that."

We continued to walk across the Downs for the next hour, hand in hand, chatting about nothing in particular, just enjoying each other's company. When it was obvious that Monty had enough, we started the short walk back to the cottage. Reaching the cottage, Mason opened the door and guided me in.

"Are you ready to eat now?"

"I'm famished. I never realised how hungry you could get just from a walk."

"Oh yeah, you can get really hungry," Mason said, pulling me to him.

Slapping him playfully on the shoulder, I replied, "Behave yourself!" as a giggle escaped my lips.

"How can you expect me to behave, when I have the most

gorgeous woman in Kings View staying at my house, especially after that kiss?"

I could feel my cheeks turning bright red from embarrassment.

"And she looks so cute when she is embarrassed. Come on, let's get some food inside you."

We walked together into the kitchen, and Mason started to get everything together for dinner.

"Is there anything I can do to help?"

"Yes, there is, actually. You can pour two glasses of wine from the fridge, sit down, and keep me company."

"That's not what I meant."

"I know what you meant, and don't worry, I have it covered. I can cook, you know. I'm not some pampered millionaire who needs a chef."

"You're a millionaire?" The shock was clear in my voice.

"Yes, I am, but don't tell my brother. He thinks I only have a few hundred thousand after buying this place."

Sitting there for a while, it finally began to sink in. I was sitting in a gorgeous millionaire's house after the best kiss of my life, all because of some stalker that wanted me for whatever reason. Lost in my thoughts, I didn't know whether to laugh or cry. Mason had obviously sensed that something wasn't right as he was now by my side, kneeling on the floor looking up at me with concern in his eyes.

"Jess, babe, what's wrong? We can take everything as slow as you like. Nothing has to go further than the kiss if you don't want it to, and we will get to the bottom of what's happening at your flat."

He placed my hands into his and rested them on my lap.

"It's not that, Mace, it's just," I paused, "It's just so overwhelming. I've gone from a small town coffee shop owner to a woman with a stalker who is staying at a gorgeous millionaire's cottage. It's just a lot to take in and at this precise moment in time, I don't know whether to laugh or cry."

"Please don't cry. It cuts me right through the heart every time I see the tears falling from your beautiful eyes. Just trust me to make things better for you, please."

"I trust you, more than I have trusted anyone in my life before. I know I keep saying it, but thank you. I couldn't have got through today without you."

Allowing a slight smile to form on my lips, Mason placed a kiss on my forehead and got up from where he was kneeling.

"Anytime, babe."

Babe. It sounded so different from Mason's lips. When Chris had called me that it felt wrong, almost creepy, but hearing Mason say it, filled me with warmth.

Sitting at the kitchen table, sipping a glass of wine, I watched as Mason expertly cooked our meal of salmon, new potatoes, and vegetables. It looked and smelled divine when he placed the plate in front of me.

"Bon Appetit."

"I could get used to this, you know."

"I hope you do."

We sat there, eating our meal, just chatting about this and that, when the question I had been expecting from Mason since his confession about his fiancé was asked.

"So, why are you on your own, Jess? Why no boyfriend or fiancé in your life, if you don't mind me asking?"

Finishing my meal, I placed my knife and fork on the now empty plate and took a sip of my wine, contemplating how I would answer that question.

"I don't know, really. Probably because I never found the right man. I have gone out with guys in the past, but always seemed to find the wrong ones. They were only after one thing and didn't like the hours I kept, so it usually ended up being a one night stand on their part. Please don't think I'm easy. It wasn't loads of guys, and they always knew how to sweet talk me around in a short space of time. I guess I'm just gullible that way."

"I would never suggest you are easy, or gullible. I'm a man, remember? I know what powers we can have over women at times."

"I bet, and I also bet you have used them once in a while as well." I gave him a playful smirk, and continued. "Anyway, after a while I was fed up with being used, so I just didn't bother anymore. Looking after the coffee shop takes up all my time, and usually after a day there, I collapse when I get home, so definitely no time for a boyfriend."

"Well, we are going to have to try and resolve that, aren't we? That is, if you would agree to go out with me as my girlfriend, for real, and not just for the sake of your stalker?"

My eyes immediately snapped up and met Mason's. I had to ask the question that was running through my head.

"Mace, did you really just ask me, Jessica Davis, to be your girlfriend?" My heart was pounding in my chest waiting for his answer and I'm sure he could hear it as a smile formed on his lips.

"Yes, but I will make it more formal if you would like. Jessica Davis, I, Mason King, would like to ask you to become my girlfriend." As he said the words he took both my hands in his and lifted them placing a kiss on each of them.

Lost for words, I sat there for a second, just looking at Mason, unable to speak from the shock of what he had just said. The smile started to fade from his face, and I could see it change to worry that I was about to say no. Squeezing his hands in mine, I finally managed to get my words out.

"MMMason, of course, I would love to be your girlfriend."

"There's a but coming here, isn't there?"

"Now who is jumping to conclusions? There is no but, I am just so overwhelmed by everything that has happened today, and now you are asking me to be your girlfriend....it's just everything I have ever wanted, to be cared for, everything I have been missing for the last few years of my life."

"Jess, I more than care for you. I know we have only really known each other for a short while, but I think I fell for you the first day I saw you at the shop. Then, when I saw how Monty reacted to you and the kindness you showed him, that was it. I was gone, no going back." After we stared at each other for another moment, he hopped up. "Let's get cleaned up in here and then we can just relax for the rest of the evening."

Insisting that I would clean up everything from dinner as Mason had cooked, he went into the living room to light a fire, as I washed and put everything away. For a bachelor, I had to admit that Mason was very tidy and had everything just in the right place. I had no trouble finding where everything went as I put it all into cupboards and drawers.

Hearing Mason walk back into the kitchen, I didn't jump this time when he spoke.

"All done?"

"Yep, everything is cleaned and put away."

"Good, the fire is lit. Did you want to grab a shower and change into something more comfortable first?"

"Sounds like my idea of heaven."

"OK, I'll show you to a room and the bathroom."

Grabbing my case on the way through, Mason led me upstairs to one of the bedrooms and placed my case down.

"The bathroom is across the way and there are towels already in there, so use whatever you need. I'll meet you back downstairs when you're done."

"OK, thanks."

Opening my case, I grabbed a pair of pyjama shorts and a cami top and placed them on the bed. I walked across into the bathroom to get cleaned up for the rest of the evening.

Walking downstairs and into the living room after my shower, I found it was exactly how I expected it to be, warm and homely. There was a fire raging in the hearth, with two, two seater leather settees, a rug, coffee table, and a TV in the corner. Monty was asleep on his bed in the corner, quite content.

Sitting down on one of the settees, I noticed that Mason had placed our two glasses of wine and what was left in the bottle on the coffee table. Mason walked in a few minutes later after obviously having a shower and changing into a pair of lounge pants and t-shirt. God, he looked sexy, I could now see his toned body and all of his rippling muscles trying to escape the tight confines of his shirt. Sitting down next to me on the settee, he pulled me close to him and placed his arm around me. Leaning into him, I thought how I could definitely get used to this every evening.

"Anything in particular you would like to watch?"

"Not really. I rarely watch TV in the evening. If I do get time to relax, I tend to just read, so anything is fine."

"OK, I'll just find a film to put on in the background then, one we don't really have to pay attention to."

Flicking around for a little while, Mason finally settled on

Jurassic World, which I must admit surprised me, when he could have chosen any action movie going.

"Good choice."

"Well, I thought you might like to watch Chris Pratt for a while, seeing as all women like him, don't they? And the film's not that bad either."

We sat there for a while, me leaning against Mason's chest while he drew circles on the top of my arm. Looking up, I saw that Mason was gazing down at me smiling.

"What?"

"Nothing, I was just sitting here, realising how lucky I was having a beautiful woman in my arms."

"You keep calling me beautiful, but why? I'm not really that special, just a normal woman with a few lumps and curves here and there."

"Jess, you are beautiful, both on the outside and on the inside. I told you before, I know the difference now. Just because you don't consider yourself to be a catwalk model, that doesn't mean you aren't beautiful, and for the record, you could be a catwalk model if you wanted."

"Mason, you could have anyone in this world you wanted. You're handsome, kind, caring, and not to mention loaded, so why me?"

"For all those reasons, Jess. You don't care that I am handsome, well at least I don't think so, and I know you don't care about how much money I have, because you kissed me before you knew I was a millionaire. I don't want someone to be with me because of my looks and money; I want someone to be with me because they care about me as a person. Much in the same way, you don't want someone to be with you just because you will sleep with them."

"You're right, I don't care about your money. You could give it all away and I would still want to be with you. I don't care what you look like, although it is a bonus you are gorgeous. You just want to protect me and care for me, and that is all I want."

"Jess, I said earlier, we can take this as slow as you want. The fact that you are here in my arms is everything to me right now. Until this moment, I hadn't realised that I wanted this, no *needed* this in my life. Having you in my arms right now, I feel complete. I thought I could live my life alone but now I realise that a part of me was empty. And you being here right now, I feel whole again.Whatever you want, I'll give it to you. Whatever you need, I will make sure you have it. As far as I'm concerned, you are my everything, my forever. I know that seems too soon, but I have never felt this happy in my entire life, the way I feel with you next to me right now."

Looking into his eyes, I was expecting to see a flicker of doubt in them, but all I could see was the truth there. He meant every word he had just said to me. In that one moment, gazing into his eyes, I knew I wanted him in my life forever as well.

"That almost sounds like a proposal of marriage, Mr. King," I said teasingly.

"I was just saying that......"

"It's fine, I get what you're saying. I feel exactly the same way. I want you as my forever as well. Right now, being here with you in your arms is all I need as well. As for taking things slowly, I think we both know what we want after that kiss."

"Jess, please don't do something because you think I want it. I don't care if you sleep in the other room or just lie in my arms all night. I can wait as long as you need. I want you, hell yes I do, but only when you want it too."

"Mason, I want you, no, I need you. I need you to make me feel alive; I haven't felt this way before about anyone in my life. Even if we don't stay together forever, I need to know what it's like to be cherished and loved by someone who loves me as much as I love him." I paused before saying, "Mace, take me to bed and make love to me."

Chapter Sixteen

Mason

That was it, it was all I needed. That confirmation that she wanted and needed me too, that she wanted to be in my bed with me, wanted me to make love to her. When I had walked back into the living room and saw her sitting there in that short and cami set, I almost lost it there and then. I wanted to drag her up to my room and make love to her all night long, but I knew I had to try and slow things down. She had to want it as much as me, and she did. Those few words telling me she was willingly giving me her body to pleasure.

Switching off the TV, I got up off the sofa and picked Jess up in my arms. Gasping, she placed her arms around my neck and leaned into my chest. Yeah, this definitely felt right having her in my arms, I thought as I carried her to my bedroom.

Stepping through the door, I carefully placed her down next to the bed. Running my hand down her body and over her breasts, I could feel her nipples tighten as a small moan left her lips. Continuing down, I grabbed the hem of her top and gently pulled it up over her body and head, giving me my first look at her naked body.

"Fucking gorgeous!" I said as I leant down and took one of her nipples into my mouth, teasing it with my tongue and finally nipping it with my teeth.

"Mason," Jess gasped, and I quickly placed my arm around her as I felt her body go weak with pleasure.

Lifting her up and gently placing her on the bed, I pulled my t-shirt over my head and took off my pants, releasing my already hard and aching cock. I needed to feel her skin against mine. Getting onto the bed and straddling her, I looked down to see her beautiful eyes full of lust. My lips crashed down onto hers, unable to wait any longer, her arms wrapped around me as she ran her nails down my back.

I could feel my heartbeat through my whole body, the blood rushing to my cock. I needed to be inside her, to feel her tight pussy pulsing around it, to feel what my body had been craving, no, needing all this time. Jess was mine and mine alone, and I was never going to let her go.

Breaking the kiss, we both gazed at each other for a second, short, panting breath escaping our lips. Leaning down, I placed soft kisses into her neck and continued down her body to her breasts, where I once again took one nipple into my mouth, sucking and nipping while I rolled the other between my thumb and finger. The soft moans coming from Jess's lips told me she liked it, and so I moved onto the other breast, taking the nipple in my mouth as I moved my hand down her body to the waistband of her shorts.

I moved down her body placing kisses along the way, pulling down her shorts trailing them along hers legs as I allowed my tongue to follow them, licking and kissing her until they had been completely removed and she was lying there, completely naked beneath me.

"Mason," Jess begged, as her hips lifted underneath me.

Gently breathing on her pussy, I could see the wetness of her arousal already forming, the smell of citrus filling my senses, utterly delicious. Softly parting her folds, I licked around her bud, causing her breath to hitch and her hips and her body to jolt at the touch. I needed to devour her, to taste her sweet nectar as she came undone for me.

Circling her swollen bud, I sucked and licked, madly circling it as her pants increased. I could feel the heat and wetness on my face increase as I continued to pleasure her. Placing one finger, then two into her, I started to thrust, hitting the sweet spot each time that I knew would make her lose herself to the pleasure.

Feeling how close she was, I added more pressure with each thrust, her wetness coating my face and hand with every flick of my tongue. Feeling her tighten around my fingers, I lifted my head to look at her and pressed her clit hard, watching as she screamed my name in pure ecstasy.

Absolutely fucking gorgeous.

Lapping up all of her sweet juices, removing my fingers and trailing them down her thighs, I watched, waiting for her to come down from her sexual high. As she opened her eyes, they immediately met mine.

"Mason," she whispered.

"Yes, babe," I said as I positioned myself over her body.

Feeling my cock gliding through her wetness, I started to lower myself down onto her.

"Mason, wait."

"What's wrong, babe? If you want me to stop, just say. I won't mind."

"No, it's just...."

"Jess, you can tell me anything, please, what's wrong?"

"It's been quite some time since I have been with anyone."

"We really don't have to ...."

"No, Mason." Her hand came up and cupped my face. "There is nothing I want more right now than feeling you inside me. Just... take it slow."

"Are you sure? It's been a while for me as well, so I'm not sure how long I can last."

"Please, Mason. I want you."

Positioning the tip of my cock at her entrance, I whispered, "Tell me if I hurt you and I'll stop."

Smiling up at me she nodded her head and closed her eyes. Slowly allowing my head to push into her folds, I felt her heat engulf my cock, causing waves of pleasure to wash over me. I had never felt like this before entering a woman. Carefully leaning down, I took her mouth into mine, kissing her passionately as I slowly pushed into her.

She was so tight. I could feel her squeezing my cock in the most delicious way, sucking me into her. I closed my eyes, savouring this moment. If this was the only time I was going to have her, I wanted to remember every second. With my cock almost fully inside her, I stopped and broke our feverish kiss. Leaning down to her ear, I whispered, "Are you OK?"

Jess opened her eyes and gazed into mine.

"Yes," she whispered as her legs wrapped around my body and she thrust her hips up towards me. *Fuck.*

I kissed her again as I slowly slid in and out of her, building up a rhythm. Each time her pussy pulled me deeper into her and the heat and wetness grew with each stroke. I couldn't describe the feeling I was experiencing right now, the pleasure rolling each time I glided into her with her pussy gripping me like a vice.

This was better than any adrenaline rush, drug, or drink that I could imagine. Any thoughts I had before of not being able to trust any women again was completely gone. Here in this moment, Jess was mine, and I was hers forever, and I was damn sure that I was going to make this forever.

Our kisses had become almost frantic as I picked up the pace and Jess moaned as I hit the sweet spot inside her. Spurred on by her moans, our pace increased; I wasn't sure how much longer I could hold on, especially as I could feel her tightening around me. We broke the kiss together, both needing to breathe.

"Jess, I don't think I can last much longer," I said as I felt my balls tighten with the pleasure of my impending orgasm.

Reaching down, I rubbed her clit with my finger, hearing her breaths and moans increase.

"Mason, I'm going to…"

I pressed down on her clit hard as I felt myself hit the point of no return. Cumming together, she screamed my name one last time, as a guttural groan came from my lips and I stopped myself from falling onto her.

Pulling out of her, I immediately felt the warmth disappear and missed it. Rolling onto one side of the bed I pulled her towards me and just held her, allowing both our breathing to return to normal. Gently stroking her hair as she rested her head on my chest, I could tell exhaustion was taking her over.

"Shhhh, Jess, get some rest. I have a feeling it's going to be a long night."

With that, we both allowed sleep to take over our bodies as we lay there in each other's arms.

Chapter Seventeen

Jessica

The sound of my alarm going off woke me, and I realised I was still in Mason's arms. So last night wasn't just a dream, it had really happened. Even if I hadn't been in his arms, the ache throughout my body would have confirmed it anyway. We had made love three times during the night and each time was more amazing than the first. To be honest, I was surprised I was actually awake. Reaching over, I switched off the alarm and tried to gently get out of Mason's arms.

"Trying to escape me already?"

Turning to face him, I found Mason lying there smiling at me.

"No, I just need to get ready for work, and I believe all of my clothes are in the guest room where I left them last night before you carried me in here."

"We will have to do something about that then, won't we? I'll go make a coffee while you grab a shower."

Placing a kiss on my forehead, he got out of bed.

"That's all you're getting for the moment, or we will never get out of here."

With that, he walked out of the bedroom. Laying there for a minute, I took in everything that had happened in the last twenty-four hours. I had a boyfriend, and not just any boyfriend, a gorgeous millionaire boyfriend, who happened to be great in bed. Prising myself out of bed, I walked over to the guest room where my case was and pulled out clothes for the day. I could sort out the rest later, and went to have a shower.

When I was suitably refreshed and dressed for the day, I walked down to the kitchen to find Mason was already showered and dressed, drinking a cup of coffee. Walking past him to get my coffee, he grabbed me round the waist and pulled me towards him, planting a generous kiss.

"Morning, babe."

"You already gave me a kiss this morning."

"Yeah, but it wasn't a proper morning kiss. If it had been, we wouldn't be ready now. How are you feeling, anyway?"

I smiled at him archly, "A little sore, but most definitely in a good way."

"Glad to hear it. We better get going, it's nearly 5:00, and I know you like to be in the shop early."

Finishing my coffee, I washed up both of our mugs and grabbed my bag from my room. Mason was already waiting for me at the door with Monty next to him.

"No, boy. You can stay here today and sleep all day, or have a party. Whatever you want to do."

Monty just tilted his head as though he understood every word that had just been said to him. Leaning down, I gave him a rub behind the ear and got a lick of thanks in return.

"I'll see you later, Monty, and if you're good, I'll bring you back some of my biscuits."

With a small bark, he ran off and went back to his bed.

"Well, that was easier than I thought."

"It was the promise of biscuits that did it."

"He has definitely taken a shine to you, but he's not getting biscuits every day, or he'll get fat. Come on, let's get going."

We walked out the door together and over to Mason's car. Always the gentleman, he opened the door for me and helped me into the car, making sure I was settled before closing the door behind me. A few moments later he was climbing in beside me. We took the short fifteen minute drive to his office and he parked the car.

It seemed strange walking down the street hand in hand with Mason. I was still thinking it was all a dream, that I would wake up at any moment and reality would set in. However, right now this was my reality. I was the girlfriend of Mason King, and I couldn't be happier.

Opening the door to the shop, I walked in with Mason behind me and switched on all the lights.

"Anything I can do to help?"

"Do you know how to use the coffee machines out front?"

"Are they normal Barista coffee machines?"

"Yep."

"Then yes, I do. What do you want?"

"A black coffee, please. And can you start getting a hazelnut latte ready for Chris? He will be knocking on the door in about twenty minutes."

"I didn't think you opened until 6:30?"

"I don't, but I have to make an exception for Chris. He helps me with things in the flat and he's my next door neighbour."

"OK, well he doesn't need to help anymore."

"Is that a hint of jealousy I hear in your voice?"

"Not at all, but I can help you now, can't I? Also, you won't want the flat for much longer if we move in together permanently."

"Don't get ahead of yourself there, Mr. King. But yes, you can help me in the flat if it makes you feel better."

"It does. I'll go and make the coffees."

Smiling to myself as he walked out to the front of the shop, I set about putting things into the oven and placing the soup into the slow cookers for lunchtime. Walking out the front with a bag of pastries for Chris, I watched as Mason expertly made the coffees.

"I think I should give you a job here. You obviously know what you're doing."

"I worked in a coffee shop for a while when I was at Uni. I had to earn some money somehow."

Passing me my coffee, he carried on making the latte for Chris. He had just put it down on the counter when there was a knock at the shop door. Going to get it, Mason stopped me.

"I will get it, Jess."

He took the keys from me and walked to the door, unlocked and opened it, allowing Chris to come inside. Chris obviously hadn't seen me standing there because his comment was one of shock.

"Who are you and what are you doing in Jess's shop?"

Immediately I saw Mason's posture change. He straightened up to his full height almost defensively.

"I'm Mason, and I'm Jess's boyfriend."

"Yeah, and I'm the King. Jess hasn't got a boyfriend, so I will ask you again, who are you and what are you doing here?"

Before I could interrupt this testosterone filled argument, Mason spoke again.

"You might not be a king, but I am! My name is Mason King, and I'm Jess's boyfriend."

Deciding it was best to break this up now, before things got out of hand, I walked up to Mason and put my arm around him. He immediately responded by doing the same.

"Chris, it's fine. Mason is my boyfriend. We only got together yesterday, so that's why you don't know yet."

There was a flicker in Chris's eyes, but I couldn't quite work out what it was. It almost looked like a combination of hurt, anger, and jealousy, but it quickly went back to neutral in a blink.

"Sorry, Mason. I just worry about Jess, and I thought you were here to hurt her. Pleased to meet you. I'm Chris Carter, and I live next door to Jess."

"Not a problem, Chris. I'm pleased to know there is someone looking out for her."

I breathed a sigh of relief that was over with; I could imagine a full scale "Bridget Jones Brawl" going on out in the street for a minute.

"I have your coffee and pastries ready for you, Chris. Do you need any lunch?"

"No thanks. I'm being taken out by a client today. Thanks for thinking of me, though."

I took the money from him for his drink and food and placed it in the till.

"I will see you in the morning, Jess. Good to meet you again, Mason."

"You too, Chris."

"Mason, make sure you hold onto her. You never know when she may decide to leave you. See ya, Jess."

"Bye, Chris."

Chris left the shop and Mason went to lock the door, then turned to look at me, the confusion as clear as mine.

"What did he mean by that? That's an odd thing to say when a couple first gets together. Is he always so negative?"

"I really have no idea. He's been acting really strange lately. Suddenly he started calling me babe. It was quite creepy. Hopefully now he knows I am going out with you, he will stop it."

"Well, let me know if he makes you feel uncomfortable again, and I will have a chat with him. Has he done anything to indicate to you that he could be involved in your harassment?"

"No. Chris has always been kind and helpful. Besides, he didn't even know that I had a brother until after this all started."

"Maybe he has just started to develop a crush?"

"Maybe, but I have never shown any interest in him. I think of him more as a friend or brother, than a lover."

"Well as I said, if you want, I'll have a word with him."

"Thank you."

"Anytime, babe. Sorry, I best stop calling you that, hadn't I?"

"No, I love you calling me that. It just sounded so weird when Chris said it, that's all."

"OK, well, anything else I can help you with?"

"I just need to make two lattes for when Mr. Duncan comes in, and you've got to wait for him as Mrs. Duncan is the biggest gossip in town. As soon as she knows, the whole town will know."

"You're happy for everyone to know about us then?"

"Of course. We were going to tell everyone we were going out together anyway. Now it's the truth, and not for the case of my stalker."

Mason walked over to me and pulled me to him. I was really starting to get used to this. He bent down and kissed me tenderly on the lips.

"How did I get so lucky?"

"What do you mean?"

"How did I end up with the most beautiful woman in Kings View?"

"Just lucky, I guess." I smiled at him. "I'm going to get the pastries out of the oven and start the second lot. Could you start getting two lattes ready for Mr. Duncan as he will be here soon."

"OK, will do."

I got everything going in the back. Stepping back out front, I stood there for a while just looking at Mason. I hadn't really noticed how well-built he was, even after spending the night in bed with him.

"Are you just going to stand there watching me?"

"Well, it is a nice view, so why not?"

Laughing, he carried on making the lattes. A knock on the door announced the arrival of Mr. Duncan. I unlocked the door, greeting him as he walked in.

"Good morning, Mr. Duncan. How are you this morning?"

"I am very well, thank you. How are you?"

"I'm good, thanks," I said walking back to the counter.

"Mason, you're here early."

"Just doing exactly as you asked me, Mr. Duncan, and taking care of Jess."

"Is he looking after you, Jess? He's not taking advantage of you, is he?"

"No, he is looking after me. You'll probably see him quite a bit more as we have started going out with each other."

"That's wonderful news. I know Mabel will be pleased. She has been hoping that you two would get together. I can't wait to tell her."

Smiling at Mason, I could tell he was thinking the same as me. The whole town would know by lunchtime, if not sooner.

"What soup do we have for lunch today, Jess?"

"Maddie made an oxtail soup for today. Would you like me to save you some?"

"Yes, please. It's been ages since I've had a homemade oxtail soup. The tin stuff isn't the same. Think I will have a beef sandwich today to go with it for a change."

"Not a problem. I will have it ready for you at your usual time."

"Thank you, my dear, and congratulations again."

"See you later, Mr. Duncan." And with that, he was gone.

"Well, the whole town will know now. Is there anything else you'd like me to do?"

"No, I just have to wait for the customers to start coming in now. Why don't you sit down with your coffee until you're ready to go to work. Are all the guys in today?"

"All except Tyler. He's on his assignment, so he can't take too much time off."

"OK, I will get coffee ready for them all just before you go."

We sat down at the table chatting about how we hoped our day would go and before we both knew it, it was 07:30.

"I best get those coffees ready."

Walking over to the counter, I started getting the coffees ready for the guys; I knew their order by heart now, they had been in so many times. Placing the four drinks into a holder, I gathered together some fresh croissants for them as well. I had to make sure I looked after them.

"There you go, all ready," I said as the first customer of the morning came through the door.

"Thanks, Jess. How much do I owe you?"

"It's fine, I have to look after you, don't I?"

"You won't make any money if you carry on like that."

"You can make up for it later. I'll have lunch ready for you guys around 12:30, if you want to send someone down to get it."

"God, a guy could fall for you so easily," he said as he gave me a quick kiss on the lips. "I'll be back around 5:00. Call me if anything funny happens."

"Will do. I'll see you later."

As he walked out the shop, I suddenly had a feeling of emptiness that he wasn't next to me. Mason King was definitely a guy that you could fall for, and the way I was feeling right now, I was falling for him big time.

Chapter Eighteen

Mason

Walking away from Jess's shop carrying the coffees and pastries she had given me, I felt a lowliness I had never felt before. It had been three years since I'd had someone in my life and didn't think I would again, but now I had Jess. And even though I had only just left her, I missed her. I meant what I had asked her. How the hell did I get that lucky? Not only was she gorgeous and great in bed, but for the first time ever I felt complete.

Walking up to the office, I saw that Jayden was already there. Strange, he never got to the office before 8:30. Stepping into the lobby, I placed all of the coffees down except for Jayden's and mine and continued into his office.

"Hey, bro, you're in early. Couldn't sleep?"

"Nah, just thought you might be late, so I got started on a few things before you got here."

There was something in his tone that sent alarm bells ringing in my head. What did he need to do before I got into the office?

"Jayden, what aren't you telling me?"

"Nothing, Mace, just getting some stuff done as I said."

"Jayden!"

"OK, have you been up to the flat this morning?"

"No, Jess and I have just been in the coffee shop getting ready for the day. Why, what's happened?"

"I had a call from Tyler last night. With everything that happened yesterday, he didn't want to worry you or Jess."

"Jayden, just get to the point."

"Well, Tyler went round to install some cameras, as you know. The problem was, there were already several cameras in Jess's flat. One in her bedroom, one in the kitchen, and another in the living room...." He paused.

"Jayden, tell me everything, please."

"There was also one in her bathroom."

"What the fuck! You're telling me that her stalker has been watching her all this time, and in the shower as well?"

"I'm sorry, bro. We thought it best not to tell you last night. It looked as though Jess was already freaked out enough, so we didn't want to add to it."

"Fair enough, but you can't keep stuff like that from me again, please. What did he do about it?"

"He decided it was best if he left them there and acted like he didn't see them. He just used the excuse that he was looking at the fuse board, using his cover story, just in case the stalker was watching. He has managed to hack into the feed so we can watch it for any glimpse of the guy. He's also hidden a sensor for movement in the flat.

The problem is, the guy is good, almost as good as Tyler. Anyone else would never have noticed them. Hell, you've been in the flat and you didn't notice them."

"To be fair, I wasn't actually looking for them. OK, so what do we do now?"

"I guess we wait. If the movement sensor is triggered, it will send a text to me and Tyler, and then one of us can check the cameras to see our stalker."

"OK, keep me posted. And Jayden, don't keep anything else from me when it comes to Jess, please."

"You've fallen for her, haven't you?"

"We have started seeing each other, if that's what you mean."

"That's not what I mean, and you know it. I saw it yesterday, we all did. You've fallen for her, Mace, and I'm happy for you. I just want to see you happy and you are."

"We just need to take things slowly, Jayden. I don't want to pressure her into anything more. But yeah, after last night, I have fallen for her. I want to be with her forever, to have her in my bed every night. I can't lose her, bro."

"We'll get to the bottom of this, and as long as she is staying with you, she will be safe. We'll all make sure of that."

"Thanks, bro, it means a lot. Here, she made you a coffee," I said, placing the coffee cup down.

"Hell, if she is sending us coffee and croissants every morning, you better not fuck this up."

Laughing at him, I walked out into the corridor and up to my office. Typical Jayden, I thought, always thinking about his stomach. If he ever finds himself a woman, she better be a good cook.

Spending the rest of the morning keeping myself busy, I tried not to dwell on the fact someone had put cameras into Jess's flat. I knew if I thought about it, I would just get angry and then she would know that something was wrong. Not realising how much time had gone by, I was quite surprised when Brandon walked in with lunch.

"Shit, is it that time already? I thought it was only about 10:00. Must be the fact I was up so early this morning."

"Whoa, I think you need to stop there. Don't need to know what you were doing this morning, Mace. I know we're close, but that would be too much information."

"Get your mind out of the gutter, Brandon. Jess has to start work at the shop at 5:00. That's why I was up so early. Although, the fact we were up half the night won't have helped."

"There you go, you had to do it, didn't you? Seriously man, I am so happy for you, your whole personality has changed overnight."

"You and Jayden were right, I did need this. Or should I say, I needed Jess? I just hope we can find out what's happening at her place before something happens to her."

"We will….."

Brandon was cut off by Jayden suddenly running into the room.

"Mace, the sensor has gone off in Jess's flat."

"OK, so why aren't you watching the feed?"

"That's the problem, this guy is better than we thought. He turned the feed off before he went into the flat. It's dead. Do you still have Jess's keys?"

"Yeah, let's go."

Grabbing Nathan on the way, we all headed out to Jess's flat. Luckily we didn't have to go past her shop to get to the back stairs. If we had, she would have known something was up. Carefully ,I walked up the stairs alone, leaving the guys downstairs waiting for my signal. If I ran into anyone, I could just say I was getting some stuff for Jess, now we were seeing each other.

Walking up to her front door, I carefully opened it and walked inside. The place was a mess, and everything had been turned over or emptied. I checked every room and whoever had been in here was gone. Whistling to the guys to come up, I walked into the kitchen and found a note on the table written in red with a knife stabbed into it.

My heart ran cold as soon as I read it.

> *Don't think your new*
> *boyfriend can save you.*
> *I can take you anytime I want*
> *and I will soon!*
> *I will kill if I have to, just like he*
> *killed my heart.*

Next to the note was the other half of the torn picture we had found yesterday, with Sean, Jess's brother standing there. I just stared at the note. I couldn't comprehend what the hell was going on.

"What the fuck, what the hell happened here?" I heard Jayden say as he and the guys walked into the room.

"Mace, you OK?" Brandon asked, as he walked up to me. He obviously read the note because the next word out of his mouth said it all.

"Fuck. Mace, we have got to get the police involved in this."

"They didn't want to know, Brandon. They put it down to a ghost for fuck's sake. It will look suspicious if we go to them now. Whoever did this obviously knows we are on to him. Why turn off the cameras? Did you get a text when I walked into the flat, Jayden?"

"Actually, come to think of it, no."

"There you go, he knows. He must have disabled the sensor, but set it off deliberately as he was leaving to make us come here. He's probably watching us right now."

"What are we going to do?" Nathan asked.

"I don't know, we need to think about this. The first note and letter came up blank for fingerprints, so I don't think there is much point sending this to him. Shit, what am I going to tell Jess?"

I could feel the anger building inside me, I really needed to calm down. Fuck, why had I given up smoking, I could really use a cigarette right now. I stood there, trying to regulate my breaths and calm myself down, when I felt a hand rest on my shoulder.

"Mace, I know you're angry, but it's not going to get us anywhere."

Brandon was always the calm one and the voice of reason.

"If I get my hands on him, Brandon, you just better hope you are there, because I will kill him. No one threatens my woman."

Whoa, where had that come from? I know we were seeing each other now, and I really cared for Jess, but my woman?

"Come on, Mace, we can go down and talk to Jess. Jayden, call the police; they should see this before we clean things up. Also, see if you can get a hold of Sean again. We need to know if there is anyone he can think of that had that much of a grudge against him to do this."

"On it, Brandon."

"Mace."

Brandon pulled me from my thoughts, as I just stood there staring at the note.

"OK, let's go, and thanks, guys."

Brandon helped me out of the flat. It was as if my legs had stopped working and my head was just in a daze. We walked down the stairs, and Brandon grabbed my arm before we could walk round the front to the shop.

"Mace, you know Jess is going to lose it when we tell her. You need to be her strength and I am not sure if you can be that at the moment. I know you're angry. Shit, I am too, but you need to put that anger to the back of your mind for the moment and be there for her. We can find someone to run the shop for her if she wants, and I can run the business if you just want to get out of here for a while."

"Thanks, I appreciate it. Once we've told her, I'll have a chat with her and find out what she wants to do."

Walking around the front, we walked into the shop to find it full of customers. Shit, this wasn't going to be easy. As if sensing something was wrong, Maddie immediately walked over to us.

"Mason, what's wrong?"

Brandon immediately answered for me. "Something has happened in Jess's flat, and we need to have a chat with her. Are you able to hold the fort while we speak? I'll fill you in after."

"No problem. Anything Jess needs. Mace, are you OK?"

"Yeah, I'm OK. And thank you, Maddie. Jess is really going to need you over the next few weeks."

"As I said, anything she needs."

"Hi, Mace, Brandon. Everything OK?"

"Hey, babe, can we have a word out back? Maddie said she will look after the shop."

"Of course. What's up? You have me worried now."

"Nothing we can't handle, Jess. Come on out back and we'll explain," Brandon said.

Placing my hand on her back, I guided Jess to the kitchen and sat down with her at the workstation. Taking her hand in mine, I nodded to Brandon to take the lead, I wasn't sure I would be able to hold it together if I told her.

"Jess, firstly I don't want you to worry. We are doing everything we can to get this stalker."

"What's happened?"

Squeezing her hand I tried to give her a little bit of comfort. Brandon was right, she was going to freak out as soon as she heard this.

"When Tyler went up to your flat last night to put in the camera's he found out that someone had already put some in your flat and was obviously watching you. So as not to cause suspicion, he left them there, but put in a motion detector and then hacked into the feed to be able to see when anyone entered the flat. Earlier today the motion detector went off, but when we checked the feed it was completely blank, so whoever is doing this must switch it off whenever they go into your flat. We have just been up there to have a look and your flat has been completely trashed."

Silence. This was definitely not a good reaction. Jess was either going into complete shock, or she was going to blow at any minute. Calmly, she spoke, her expression completely blank.

"There's more you're not telling me, isn't there Brandon?"

Brandon looked over to me, I nodded telling him to carry on.

"There was a note with the other half of the photo we found before. It said, 'Don't think your new boyfriend can save you. I can take you anytime I want and I will soon! I will kill if I have to, just like he killed my heart.'"

I could feel her starting to lose it, her hand was shaking in mine, and when I looked over I could see the tears starting to fall. Pulling her into my arms, I held her as the tears and sobs fell from her lips.

"It's OK, babe, I'm here. I'm not letting anyone take you from me."

"Mason, he is threatening to kill someone now, and I'm sure that's you. I don't think I could live with myself if that happened."

"Plenty of people have tried to kill me, Jess, and they haven't succeeded yet. I'm not going to let one person succeed just when I've found you. Come on, let me take you home. I can ask one of the guys to help Maddie out and lock up for you."

"I can't let him get to me. He is not going to ruin my life just because of some argument he has with my brother. No, I will stay here and you can pick me up later. He's not going to try anything with a shop full of witnesses, and Maddie will stay until you come to get me. What's happening about my flat? I'll need to go and clean it up."

"We had to call the police, just in case. As soon as that's done, Jayden and Nathan will clean the place up for you. It might take a month to find anything, but at least it will be tidy," Brandon replied with a chuckle. "I'm going to see how they are getting on now. I'll see you in a bit, Mace."

"Thanks, Brandon."

Sitting there, I held Jess in my arms. Brandon was right, I needed to be her strength, and holding her right now I could see how much this had affected her, and I was damned sure I was going to make her feel safe again, if it was the last thing I did.

Chapter Nineteen

Jessica

After a long conversation and a lot of tears, I finally managed to convince Mason that I was OK and could carry on at the shop for the afternoon. Thankfully, Brandon had quietly explained everything to Maddie, so I didn't have to go through it all again. It was 3:30 and all of the customers had left the shop, so I was out back getting everything ready for the morning.

Mason had suggested that I shut the shop for a few days, but I soon put pay to that. There was no way I was allowing this stalker to dictate my life to me. If I was going down, then it would be with a fight. Finishing up, I walked out to find Maddie sitting at her usual table with her latte and mocha for me.

"Thought you could use some comfort and caffeine, so mocha it was."

"Thanks, Maddie. I know I've said it before, but I really don't know what I would do without you. I'm also not going to take no for an answer. I am going to start paying you for all the work you do around here."

"Jess, you really don't need….."

"No, Maddie, I do, and I'm sure Mason would agree with me."

"We'll discuss it at the end of the week, OK?"

"OK."

"So anyway, how are you and Mason getting on? Are you actually seeing each other now, or is it just for the sake of your stalker?"

"No, we are going out together now. Maddie, he is amazing, I can't really explain how he makes me feel, and no, I am not going into the juicy details."

"Jess, come on, I haven't had sex in like forever. OK, it is forever, so you've got to dish the dirt."

"What! Did I just hear you right? Did you just say you have never had sex?"

"Out of that whole sentence you picked up on that."

"Of course I picked up on that. What did you expect me to do?"

"Fair play. OK, well it's not strictly true. I have once, but it's not something I can talk about, not yet, anyway. Guess I just haven't found the right guy to try again, but I do have my eyes on one."

"Do you want me to have a word with him?"

"Who?"

"Tyler, of course. You haven't really hidden that you fancy him, and I'm sure he likes you too."

"Thanks for the offer, but I'm not sure I want a relationship right now. But if I need some help I will let you know."

We sat there chatting for the afternoon, stopping every now and then when a customer came through the door, but being nearly

5:00, they were few and far between. The bell on the shop door rang, and both Maddie and I looked up to see Mason walking through the door.

"Hey, babe, you OK?"

"Yeah, I'm OK. Maddie has been doing a good job of distracting me for the day."

"Thanks, Maddie. I really appreciate you looking after Jess."

"Anytime. You never know, I might call in the favour one of these days."

"Just say the word, and I will do anything I can to help or make it happen."

"You might just regret saying that," I said with a smirk on my face.

"Right, I'm going to head off, just have a few bits left on my final dissertation to finish and then I can submit it. Once that's done, I can be all yours, Jess. Same time tomorrow morning or do you want me in a bit earlier so I can take over from Mason?"

"That would be great if you could," Mason replied.

"I will be there just before 8:00 then. See ya in the morning."

"See ya, Maddie."

With that, she left Mason and I alone in the shop. Mason pulled me into a hug, just holding me, comforting me. He didn't need to say a word, his actions said everything, and he was worried about me, wanting to take all the hurt away. Eventually he broke the silence.

"How are you actually doing, you bearing up?"

"I'm just numb, Mace. I don't think I can take this all in. I really don't understand what I have done to deserve this."

"We will find out, but until then, I don't want you on your own anywhere. Not in your flat, here, or even at my place. Whoever is doing this is starting to lose it. Your flat proved that today. He is obviously angry over something, and the fact that we are now seeing each other must have tipped him over the edge."

"I'm not going to argue with you. If I'm honest, this has scared the hell out of me. What kind of mess is my flat in?"

"The guys have tidied it up now that the police have taken all the evidence and photos they need. I don't think they will find anything, though. This guy is good; he didn't leave any fingerprints on the notes or pictures. However, he is getting help from someone, and I think it is someone at the police station. That's why I got Jayden to call our friend up at the Met. I know I can trust him; he's looking into everything for me. Anyway, enough doom for one day. Anything you need me to do before you shut up shop today?"

"Nope, Maddie and I had everything covered and are ready for tomorrow morning. Take me home, please."

Smiling at me, he took my hand and led me out the front door, locking it as we went. Just as we were about to walk up to his car, Mrs. Duncan came out of her shop.

"Jess, Mason, I'm glad that I caught you. Is everything OK? I was upstairs earlier and saw a lot of activity in your flat."

This was the one thing I didn't want because a) I didn't want them worrying about me or their own flat and b) if I told her it would be all over town in a shot. Thankfully, Mason took the initiative before I could.

"Everything is fine, Mrs. Duncan. Jess has just got an electrical problem so we had to get some people around to have a look at it. Nothing for you or Mr. Duncan to worry about. I promised I would look after her, and I am."

"Good to hear, Mason. And I am so pleased you two are going out together now. It's lovely to see you both finally happy."

"Thank you. We are very happy."

"Good, well, I will let you both get on. I will pop in to see you tomorrow, Jess."

"Look forward to it."

She turned and went back into her shop as Mason and I walked up to his car. I knew Mrs. Duncan coming round would be a reason for her to find out all the juicy gossip, but I knew Maddie and I would be able to cover it.

"Thank god I asked for the forensics to turn up in work clothes and not uniforms. I didn't want to cause that kind of worry and suspicion."

"What about the cameras, though? Won't the stalker have seen them turn up and doing their forensic work?"

"We've been monitoring them, and they are still switched off. He's either changed the frequency, blocked us, or just hasn't switched them back on. However, my friend at the Met has installed a couple of high tech ones that even Tyler couldn't get hold of. The stalker won't see them and won't be able to detect them, so if he goes back in we will see him and so will my buddy."

"That's reassuring to know."

"I just want you to feel safe again, Jess."

"Well, you're doing that right now," I said looking down at our hands.

Walking around the corner to Mason's office, we saw Jayden and Nathan just locking up.

"Hey, bro, we were just leaving. You want us to lock up?" Mason nodded. "Hi, Jess. How are you doing?" I was quite taken aback when Jayden walked up to me and gave me a hug. Looking over at Mason, I thought he was going to hit his brother in the face.

"Don't sweat it, bro. I've got to give my new bestie a hug," he laughed, "especially as she brought me cake."

"I'm fine, Jayden, and thanks for the hug. Although, it might take me a while to calm your brother down."

"Nah, he'll be fine in a minute."

"You try that again, and you'll find out how calm I can be."

"It's fine, honestly. You'll have to get used to it, I suspect."

"I know, but not after the day we've had."

"Sorry, I didn't think. I'll limit the hugs to good days. Anyway, I want to get home, so I'll see you tomorrow. Any problems, I'll send you a text."

"OK, see you in the morning, and thanks for today. You too, Nath."

Jayden and Nathan both lifted their hands in response and got into Jayden's car, driving off a few minutes later. Mason guided me over to his car and opened the door as usual, helping me in. He got in, and we started our drive home.

We sat in silence for the entire drive home. There wasn't any reason to chat. I just wanted to get in, have a long, hot shower, something to eat, and then to cuddle up on the settee again with Mason. Getting out of the car, with Mason's help again of course, he took my hand and we walked up to the door.

"Just a word of warning. Monty will probably jump right at you. He's usually quite excited to see me."

"Well, it's a good thing I have the perfect thing to make him sit then, isn't it?"

"You brought him more biscuits?"

"Well, I did promise if he was a good boy, and I can't go back on my promises to Monty now, can I?"

"God, he is going to be spoiled worse by you than Mum!"

He opened the door and sure enough, Monty came bounding up to Mason landing two paws on the top of his legs. With a little bark, he got down and sat directly in front of me, looking up with his tail wagging.

"He's wrapped around my little finger, just like his owner." I got him a biscuit out of my bag and gave it to him. One bark later, he had taken the biscuit and ran back into the house. Shaking his head, Mason just guided me into the house after him. We walked into the kitchen and I immediately set about making a coffee while Mason gave Monty his dinner.

"I know I said that I didn't want you in the house on your own, but did you want to stay here while I take Monty for his walk?"

"No, I think it would be good to go out for a walk, even if it is just to unwind. I'll go and get changed into something a bit more comfortable, though."

"No problem, I'll meet you down here in a bit."

Walking upstairs, I got changed and headed back downstairs to find Monty waiting at the front door. I sat down in the living room waiting for Mason to come down the stairs. Monty immediately ran over to me and sat down placing his head onto my knee. They say that dogs always know when something is wrong and try to give you some comfort; well looking at Monty now, I would say that's true.

Patting his head brought me some calm, exactly what I needed right now. I was completely oblivious to Mason, who had now come downstairs and was currently standing in the living room door watching me and Monty.

"The pair of you look quite at home there, do you even want to go out, Monty?"

A quick bark indicated that wasn't the case, as he got up and walked over to Mason. We walked for thirty minutes before going back to the cottage, where again, Mason refused to allow me to cook. Sitting on the settee after eating, just being in Mason's arms, I was finally able to relax. Before I knew it, I had fallen into a deep sleep.

Chapter Twenty
Chris

So I was right, she had involved King Investigation in my little plan. Foolish woman, if she thought a bunch of guys in suits could protect her, she was sorely mistaken. I had been planning this for seven years now. There was no way I was going to let her slip through my fingers like Nicola had.

I gave her everything, anything she could ever want in life and how did she repay me? She told me we were over and went off with Sean Davis. She said I was overbearing, manipulative and abusive, that I was making her life a misery. Well, what did she expect? When I tell her to do something, I expect her to do it. It's not my fault that she didn't agree and paid the consequences.

She was my whole world and that bastard took her away from me. I would make him pay; if I couldn't have Nicola, then I would take the only other love of his life, his sister Jessica. I also wouldn't be as nice to her as I was Nicola. She would pay for her brother's crime. Jess and I had been getting somewhere. She loved it when I called her babe. I could see it in her eyes. And then

Mason came along with his money and good looks.

Or was it just a cover up? Yeah, that was it. They weren't really going out together, and it was just to throw me off my game. He doesn't care about her at all, just posing as her boyfriend to draw me out. Shit, I had gone too far with the flat today. I had been so angry when that guy had been in there putting up that sensor.

He must have found my cameras; he was definitely good, but not as good as me. I had seen him on them, looking around for places to put a camera to catch me. So I took action, but it was too much. I should never have wrecked the flat, but I was just so furious at her.

I had to rethink my plan. It was obvious that she wouldn't stay in the flat on her own now, if at all. Somehow I had to get her from the shop, but if Mason was going to be there every morning, that was going to be difficult. I had to get him away somehow, get him to go somewhere he would have to stay overnight, but where?

I pulled out my phone. I needed to get things moving and had to make sure everything was in place.

"Is the place ready?" I asked as soon as he answered the phone.

"All set. The house is wired and I've sorted out the basement, just as you asked."

"Good, we'll be going ahead soon. Make sure there is food in the place. I don't want to starve while I'm held out. You've dealt with all the paperwork? I don't want it to be traced to me."

"All done, that's what you're paying me for. You know how good I am, that's why you hired me."

"We'll see about that. Just wait for my call and be ready. As soon as I get the chance, I'm taking her, but I might need you to get ahold of one of your contacts. We have a complication."

"What's that?"

"It's not what, but who. Mason King. He's currently investigating what I've been doing in the flat. I was hoping she would come to me, seeing as I paid off Detective Jenkins to ignore her request, but obviously she went to King's."

"Shit, Mason King is involved! You do know who he is, don't you?"

"Yeah, some suit who thinks he's a private investigator. I can take him down with one hand tied behind my back."

"Good luck with that. Mason King is ex SAS, along with his best friend Brandon. His brother and the other guys that work with him are also ex-military. Fuck Chris, this is bad, really bad."

"I don't pay you to tell me what's bad, just sort it out. I need Mason away from Jess for the night. Get someone to set a meeting up with him, somewhere where he will have to stay overnight. That's when I'll get her and bring her to the house."

"OK. I'll get it sorted and let you know."

"You do that."

With that I hung up the phone. Ex SAS my arse, nothing about him screamed ex-military, except for the build, he wasn't the type. He must have the wrong guy. No, nothing was going to stop me from putting my plan into action. Just a few more days and I would have her under my roof to do with as I pleased.

She might not like it at first, but in the end she would realise it was inevitable and would love me for everything I did for and to her. We would have to move away, but for the moment my gran's old house would be fine, especially now all the paperwork had been transferred to a dummy letting agent.

No one would suspect anything, and they wouldn't be able to trace it. The place was in the middle of nowhere, so there wouldn't be any prying eyes or nosey neighbours investigating any screams they might hear, and there would be screams. I loved to hear a woman scream. The thought that I had that power over them was a real turn on.

God, I wanted her, wanted her under my control. The prostitutes I had been seeing served a purpose, but I couldn't control them like I would be able to do to Jess. Once I had her at the house, she would be mine, and unlike Nicola, she would do exactly what I wanted because she wouldn't have the choice.

However, just that wasn't enough. I needed to hurt her brother as well, and the only way to do that was to send him pictures of her. I had found his email address through a friend and had a fake account set up ready to send them to him. Again, it couldn't be traced, but it would have the desired effect, and he would go mad trying to find her. My greatest wish would be to have Nicola as well, both her and Jess in the same room together. Now that would be a dream come true.

With all these thoughts going through my head, I needed to release some of the tension and frustration I was feeling, and I knew exactly where to find it, she always made me feel good when I feel like hell. Dialling her number, I waited for her to answer the call,

"Heaven, normal time, normal place?"

"See you then."

Chapter Twenty-One

Mason

We made it to Sunday without any more strange happenings at Jess's flat. I wasn't sure if that was good news or the calm before the storm. However, I was worried. I had to leave tonight for a meeting tomorrow morning in Birmingham with a possible client that wouldn't travel down to London. I didn't want to leave Jess alone, but the contract would be long term and worth millions to us.

Jess of course had told me that I had to go, that my business was just as important as her. After speaking to the guys, who promised they would keep an eye on Jess, and Maddie who said she could stay at her place, I agreed to go. But I was damn sure I would be coming back immediately after the meeting. One night away from Jess was one night too many.

Being Sunday, it was my weekly trip to my parents; I had spoken to my Mum and arranged to have dinner at 5:30. That allowed Jess to keep the shop open until 4:00 and then get changed and ready to go. We were both quite nervous. I was just hoping that my parents liked her as much as I did. Jess was just feeling like a teenager being taken to meet the parents for the first time.

Jayden, for once, had been great. He agreed to be there as well, a buffer between Jess and our Mum. I knew as soon as Mum met Jess, she would be trying to arrange shopping trips, coffee mornings and the odd mention of weddings and grandchildren. I had tried to warn Jess what she would be like, but I don't think words would do it; she really had to see it herself.

I walked into the shop just before 4:00 p.m. and found Jess and Maddie sitting in their usual spot in the front of the shop. For the first time in ages Jess was smiling. It warmed my heart to see her happy. I hated seeing the worry on her face all the time. Maddie was the first to see me.

"Shhh, lover boy has just turned up. Hey, Mason. How are you today?"

"Lover boy, eh Maddie? Is that my new nickname?"

"Well, it's better than chicken salad baguette guy."

"What?"

Jess cut in, "It's a long story and I'll tell you sometime."

"I'll look forward to that. You nearly done?"

"All finished, just waiting for you."

"Good, let's get out of here. Maddie, I'll drop Jess off at your place later. Are you both sure you won't stay at mine? Jayden will look after you both."

"We will be fine, Mace. Maddie and I will take care of each other."

"I'm still not happy about this."

"Mace, we're going to have a wild party and invite loads of strippers round. We'll be fine."

"Maddie, you're not helping," Jess said, seeing the expression on my face.

"I think I best leave now. I'll see you both later." Maddie giggled as she picked up her bag and left the shop.

"We really aren't planning a wild party. She is just winding you up, and from the look on your face, she did a good job. Come on, let's get this dinner over with."

"You're really worried about meeting my parents, aren't you?"

"Honestly, yes. I'm sure you would be feeling the same if it was my Dad and Edith."

"Yes, I would, but that is for entirely different reasons. Your Dad would be judging me to see if I was good enough for his little girl."

"And your parents won't be doing the same?"

"You'll be fine. Honestly, my parents will love you. They always wanted a daughter, so that is exactly what you will be treated like, the daughter they never got. Hell, Mum will be inviting you round for coffee all the time and asking you to go shopping with her within minutes."

"Well, we won't find out sitting here. Come on, we best go. Is it still OK to go home and get changed first? I also need to pick up a few bits for tonight and tomorrow."

"We have plenty of time, and Mum won't moan too much if we're late. I did explain that you ran a coffee shop, so it did depend on how busy you were."

Guiding Jess out of the shop, we locked up and went back to my place for Jess to get ready, pick up some stuff, and grab Monty. An hour later we were pulling into my parents' drive to find Jayden was already here, the relief clearly visible on Jess's face.

"Are you ready for this?"

"As ready as I'll ever be. Come on, I can see the curtain twitching already." A smile lit up her face.

Walking round, I opened the door for her and helped her out of the car before walking to the boot and letting out Monty. He ran up to the front door which immediately opened. Yeah, Mum had been watching us. Taking Jess's hand in mine and giving it a squeeze, we walked up to the front door where my Mum was waiting for us.

"Hi, Mum." I pulled her into a hug.

"Mason, it's good to see you, and this must be Jessica. It's lovely to meet you, my dear."

"Good afternoon, Mrs. King. It's lovely to meet you too, and please call me Jess. Jessica makes me sound so old."

"Jess it is, and you can call me Joan or Mum, whatever you are comfortable with."

"I think I have been brought up exactly the same as Mason. I have always been taught to address my elders as Mr. and Mrs. as a mark of respect."

"Good to hear, my dear. But in this case, Joan will be fine. After all, you will be my daughter-in-law soon."

"Mum, don't get ahead of yourself already."

"Oh shhh, Mason. You have not brought a young lady round to see us since that piece of trash, so it must be serious."

I went to speak, but was saved by my brother and dad walking into the hallway.

"Jess, my favourite bestie. I see you've met Mum." He walked up to Jess and gave her a hug, laughing at the same time. "Chill, bro."

"Jess, I assume from how my son has just greeted you, you prefer Jess to Jessica," Dad said.

"Nice to meet you, Mr. King. And yes, Jess is perfect."

"And as Joan has probably already argued with you, you can call me Edward or Ted. We will leave Dad for the moment." He walked up to Jess and gave her a hug. "It's great to meet you and know someone is finally making my boy happy."

"Let's get you a coffee. I'm sure you're worn out after working all day."

"That would be great, thank you, Joan. Do you need any help with dinner?"

"Oh, she is definitely a keeper, Mason. No, I am fine, thank you, my dear. I have everything under control. Mason didn't say you were vegetarian, so it's roast chicken. I hope that's OK."

"That will be wonderful. I don't know the last time I sat down to a roast dinner on a Sunday. It must be at least six years."

"Oh my God, we will have to change that. Boys, dinner will be at 5:30 every Sunday so Jess can join us, no excuses."

Smiling, I led Jess into the kitchen and we sat around the table chatting while Mum busied herself with the dinner. It was so nice to have this, to be a family. And, the fact that my parents had made Jess feel so welcome made me so happy.

After dinner, Dad suggested we go for our usual walk. I had guessed he would do this. I could tell he wanted to speak to me about Jess alone. As usual, I asked Mum and Jayden if they wanted to come and as usual they declined. Turning to Jess I asked, "Do you want to come along with us?"

"No, I will be fine here with your Mum and Jayden. I am sure your Dad wants some alone time with you to ask all the questions he is itching to ask. I will try and keep the scheduling of coffee mornings to a minimum," she said with a laugh.

"Please do. Mum will add in the afternoon teas as well if she could."

Giving her a quick kiss on the cheek, I had to keep it PG in front of my parents, I followed Dad out the door with Monty in tow.

"Say what you want to say then, Dad. I can see you have been eager to get me on my own."

"Mason, it's not like that at all."

"Isn't it?"

"OK, yes, it is. Mason, she's perfect for you. You know I never really liked Cassandra. She was just a money grubbing bitch. Excuse the language, but she was. Jess truly cares about you. I knew that as soon as she walked through the door.

Jayden had done his best to put us both at ease, saying how much she looked after all the guys, but I couldn't be sure until I met her myself, and now I'm sure. I can see why you have fallen for her. Heck, if I was your age, I would have done the same."

"Thanks, Dad. That means a lot to me. It is early stages, and she has a lot going on in her life at the moment, we both have. I can really see us married with kids, just not yet. We need to grow into that, and I don't want to rush things, but I'm also not going to let her go easily."

"Don't let her go, Mason. Women like your Mum and Jess do not come along very often, you know that. Now you have her, make her truly yours. The difference in you this week is amazing. Jayden called a few days ago and we chatted. He said the atmosphere in the office had completely changed since you met Jess, as though they didn't have to walk on eggshells around you anymore."

"I obviously need to have a chat with my brother."

"You might want to add Brandon in on that chat as well."

"What! You spoke to Brandon as well?"

"You know your Mum and I see Brandon as another son. Of course I spoke to him."

I knew they both loved Brandon, the fact he had saved my life just compounded the fact. I had saved him a few times as well, but that was always forgotten. We walked together in silence, both of us just happy to be in each other's company and to have some time away from Mum. We both loved her to bits, but she could be too much at times. I just hoped she wasn't giving Jess a hard time.

Walking back to the house a little while later, we walked in to find Jess and Mum, sitting there laughing their heads off with what looked like an extremely grumpy Jayden. Oh no, this wasn't good, I thought as I saw the photo album in my Mum's hands.

"Mace, will you tell her to put that away. I don't think I can take much more."

"Mum, what are you doing?"

"Oh good, you're back. Right, Jess. Now we can go onto the pictures of Mason. He was such a good boy as a child, but then he grew up."

"Mum, really."

"Your turn, bro."

"Jayden, don't be upset. You were an adorable baby. Really, you were." Jess said, with tears of laughter running down her face.

This is what I needed to see. Jess was happy, and the fact that my Mum had done that to her was even better. Deciding I could take some embarrassment, even if it was just to see Jess happy, I sat down in the armchair opposite my Mum and Jess.

"Let's get this over with."

"Oh don't be so glum, Mason. You knew this was going to happen one day, and I'm sure you can get your own back by looking at baby photos of Jess, when you go to visit her Dad and Edith," Mum replied.

God, what had I missed? Dad looked at me puzzled as well. How much had they got to know each other in such a short space of time? I had only found out about Edith a couple of days ago when we had sat down for a chat, and Mum had only been with Jess an hour.

Sitting there for the next hour, Jess still crying with laughter at all the pictures and stories my Mum was telling her, was probably one of the best hours of my life. Even Jayden lightened up after a little while, but that was probably at my expense. Seeing Jess relaxed and not worrying about anything was perfect, and I couldn't thank Mum enough. Once everything was over, I would tell them both, but for the moment it was best they didn't know.

Seeing it was nearly 8:00 p.m., and I really needed to get on the road to Birmingham, I interrupted my Mum at an opportune moment.

"Well, even though this has been fun, and I use that in the loosest term, we need to be heading off. I have a meeting first thing in Birmingham tomorrow and I need to drive up this evening."

"OK, son. And Jess, thank you for making him happy again," my dad said, pulling her into another hug.

"Jess, I will give you a call in the week for when I'm popping down to the coffee shop. We can have a good natter in between customers."

"I would like that, Joan. And thank you, Edward. It has been lovely meeting you both, and thank you for the lovely dinner."

"That is not a problem, my dear. You are welcome anytime, with or without our son."

"Thank you. Jayden, will I see you tomorrow?"

"Yeah, I'll pop round early to make sure you're OK and get the coffees for the guys. Call me if you need me." He gave her a hug. I was starting to get used to that, but he better not push it.

"Thanks, bro. You staying at my place with Monty?"

"Yeah, we're going to have a full on bachelor party, aren't we, boy?"

"Jayden, there are biscuits in his cupboard for him. He has one before he goes to bed."

I looked over at her. "So that's why he's so good in the evenings now. You're bribing him!"

Her smile said it all, and I just had to laugh.

"I'll give you a call in the week, Mum."

"You make sure you do."

We all said our goodbyes and I drove Jess back to Maddie's flat. I really wished she would have stayed with my brother, but she was adamant that she and Maddie would be fine. Saying goodbye was the hardest thing I had done for a long while. Part of me wanted to cancel the meeting because something didn't feel right, but I couldn't put my finger on it. However, if this was genuine, then it would set us up for a long while and I could take on some new staff.

Making sure everything was OK with Maddie, and promising I would call Jess as soon as I arrived, I set off on the two hour drive to Birmingham. The sooner I got this over with, the sooner Jess would be back in my arms.

Chapter Twenty-Two
Mason

I had arrived in Birmingham last night just after 10:00 p.m. and called Jess as soon as I got into my room. We chatted for a bit, but conscious that she had to be at work early this morning, I let her get to bed. Sleep didn't come easy to me last night. I missed her, missed having her body next to mine. It had nothing to do with the sex. I just needed to feel her next to me.

Looking at the clock, I saw it was nearly 5:00 a.m., and I knew that she would be up, so I called her. She picked up after two rings, almost as if she was waiting for my call.

"Hey, babe. How are you doing?"

"Missing you. I hardly slept without you next to me. Maddie's great, but not to cuddle up to."

"Now that's putting images into my head I'm sure I shouldn't be having."

"Mace, get your mind out of the gutter."

Jess put me on hands free and we spoke to each other while she was getting everything ready in the shop. She said she couldn't wait to see me later, and that we should just have a night in front of the fire again, but this time she would try not to fall asleep.

Hearing a knock on the front door, I guessed that Chris had arrived, and after hearing Jess check and unlock the door, I could hear him in the background.

"I'll let you go then, babe. I'll give you another call just before my meeting. Miss you."

"Miss you too, Mace. Speak later."

With that she hung up the phone. I felt better having spoken to her again, and I decided that I would try and grab a couple of hours sleep before getting ready for the meeting. Placing my head down on the pillow, thoughts of Jess running through my head, I closed my eyes and drifted off to sleep.

The ring tone on my phone jolted me from my sleep, and I looked over at the clock reading 6:45. Who in the hell was calling me this early? Picking up the phone and seeing Jayden's caller ID, I answered it.

"This better be good. I was just having some well-earned sleep before my......."

"Mason, have you spoken to Jess this morning?"

I immediately woke up properly at the tone in his voice.

"Yeah, we chatted until about 5:30 this morning, why?"

"She's not in the shop. Maddie came down at 6:30 and found the shop locked up, so she called me, knowing I had a set of keys. When we got in we saw that the pastries were burnt and Jess was nowhere to be found."

"Shit, I'm on my way back. Fuck the meeting. We need to know what's happened to her Jayden. Have you checked the surveillance camera that was installed?"

"I have Tyler working on it now. He contacted Mr. Jarvis and explained he has a personal emergency, so he may not be in for a couple of days and is heading down as soon as he watches the footage."

"OK, how's Maddie?"

"Understandably upset. We had to let the Duncans know, so the whole town will know by now."

"Fuck!"

"Mace, calm down. You can't help Jess if you're dead. You need to be careful driving home. I don't want to have to tell Mum and Dad they've lost both you and Jess."

"I should have been there, Jayden. I shouldn't have let her talk me into coming up here."

"No point thinking about it now, bro. Let's just focus on finding her and getting her back, OK?"

"I know, bro, but I just can't help thinking if I'd have been there...."

"Until we know who we are dealing with, there isn't much we can do."

"OK, I'm getting dressed and then heading back. I will call the new client on the way down and explain the situation. Hopefully they will understand. See you in a couple of hours"

"Mace, be careful, please."

"Will do, and update me with anything as you find it out."

"Sure thing. Brandon and Nath are on their way here as well. Love you, bro."

"Love you too, Jayden."

The anger and pain was radiating through me as I rushed out

of the hotel. I had gotten ready and packed in five minutes flat, most of which while I was talking to Jayden. I needed to be back in Kings View trying to find Jess. I could not live without her. I loved her. My thoughts suddenly stopped. I loved her. I hadn't even realised it. I knew I cared about her deeply, but when did that change to love, or had it always been love and I was too naïve to realise it?

The pain in me was surging throughout my body. The last time I had felt like this was when I saw the pictures of Cassandra, but this was different. This was hurt about losing someone I loved, not because of something she had done.

If only I had told her. I needed to find her, to hold her again and tell her how much I loved her, and that I was never going to leave her again, that I wanted her in my arms forever. How I was actually managing to drive the car at the moment was beyond me. If I didn't get pulled over by the police or a speeding fine I would be surprised.

Seeing it was nearly 8:00a.m., I called the number for the client I was meant to meet. Nothing, completely dead. I checked the number again. It was the one I had programmed into my phone when they had called me. Trying it again, the same thing happened. My heart sank at the thought that this was a set up. Whoever had done this needed me away from Jess and had set up a fake meeting. Forwarding the number onto my contact at the Met, I called his number.

"Mace, what do you need? Jayden filled me in, and I'm on my way down there now."

"I just sent you a number; can you try and trace it for me?"

"Will do. See you soon, Mace."

It was 8:30 when I arrived at Jess's shop and found all the guys there, but something was wrong. I could see it in their faces as I walked in. The room went silent, and they all turned to look at me. Brandon just walked over to me and put his hand on my shoulder.

"Mace, I think you best sit down."

"Brandon, what the hell? Tyler, if you are here, why didn't you call me with an update?"

"Mace, sit down now, man. I don't want to have to make you, but I will. Believe me, you are going to need to."

"Brandon, just tell me."

"It was Chris!"

As realisation dawned on me with what he had just said, I felt my legs give way underneath me. Two arms caught me and Brandon and Jayden sat me down on a chair.

"Maddie, can you make Mace a black coffee please?"

The room was spinning and I couldn't focus on anything. Someone placed the coffee mug in front of me on the table and then Brandon was in front of me, trying to snap me out of my trance.

"He arrived as I was talking to her. He knew I was speaking to her, and he took her from me. Why?"

As I was speaking, Jayden's phone started to ring.

"Jayden King. Oh, hi, Sean. Wait a second. I'm going to put you on speaker phone. There you go."

"Jayden, I understand you have been trying to get ahold of me, what's up?"

"Sean, this is Mason King here."

"Hi, Mason. I understand you've started seeing my sister. You better be…"

"Sean, sorry to cut you off, but Jess has been taken, and I think it might have something to do with you. Do you know a guy called

Chris Carter?"

"Please do not tell me he is involved."

"I'm afraid he is. What can you tell us about him? Anything that could help lead us to him and Jess?"

"Wait a second. Let me get Nicola here as well. He was her last boyfriend, and she'll be able to tell you more. But Mason, I have to warn you, it's not pretty."

For the next thirty minutes, Nicola explained to us all about her relationship with Chris, and Sean was right. It wasn't pretty. How she had survived it and came out a fully functioning person amazed me. Given the emotional, verbal, and physical abuse she suffered, she was lucky to be alive. Part way through, Callum from the Met had turned up and heard most of the explanation. Sitting there for a moment, it started to make sense.

"Chris blames you, Sean, and wants to get back at you. It all makes sense now, the note, and what he said to me when I first met him. He said that I should make sure I hold onto her, that you never know when she may decide to leave you. He's obviously been planning this for a while."

"I'm not to blame, though. He is."

"He doesn't see it that way though, Sean. As far as he's concerned, he had a great relationship with Nicola. Just because she didn't see it that way and left him, in his mind, you made her leave, not his actions."

"That's just fucked up."

"I know, Jayden, but he is obviously unstable and has some kind of mental condition. Jess said he tried the same with Maddie, but luckily Maddie was strong enough to tell him no, so he gave up. Nicola, is there anywhere you think he might take Jess?"

"Well, there is our old house, but I guess he would have sold that. The only other place I can think of is his Gran's old house, but I've only been there once and was blindfolded when he took me. That was when I realised just how sick he was. Fuck, I really hope she isn't there."

"Why, Nicola?" I asked, but didn't really want to hear the answer.

"He built a dungeon in the basement."

That was it. That was all I could take. I flung over the table in front of me, sending the coffee cup flying, and stormed out of the shop. I couldn't hear any more. I just couldn't handle it. Brandon followed me out and grabbed me into a hug. Neither of us was usually like this, but he knew I needed it. We were brothers in arms to the end, no matter what, and we looked out for each other.

"Mace, we will find her, but I really need you to get your head straight. This will get you killed if you don't put your emotions aside. This is just another mission, man. That's how you've got to look at it."

"Brandon, I love her man. I can't be without her. It will kill me inside, and I won't come back from this without her. I didn't even get the chance to tell her."

"I know, Mace, but we will find her. Callum is talking with Nicola now and getting as much information as he can. We have the whole Met behind us now. We will find her."

"Yeah, but what state will she be in? What the hell is he going to do to her in the meantime?"

"Let's deal with that when the time comes. For now, you need to think clearly and logically. You've trained for this, so pull it back from the depths where you have hidden it all this time."

"You're right, Brandon. I'm sorry, it's just…"

"You don't need to say it, Mace. I would probably be a damn sight worse if this was the other way round. Come on, let's see what they have worked out."

Calming myself down, I walked back into the shop to find Callum just hanging up his phone.

"Mace, good to see you, just wish it was under better circumstances."

"You too, Callum. Forgive me for foregoing the pleasantries."

"No problem. You know I understand better than most. I've got my guys searching the records for a house that was in the name of Greta Carter. I'm guessing he'll have transferred ownership to try and cover his tracks, but he will not be expecting my team to be involved, and if necessary, I can contact MI5 to help."

"I appreciate it, Callum. Sorry if this is dragging up bad memories."

"It's fine, Mace. I know you didn't mean for this to happen. I had hoped we would work this out before we got here, but we will find her. Do you know where this Chris lives?"

"Yeah, he lives in the flat next to Jess, upstairs."

"OK, let's go have a look. I suggest you keep the shop closed for the moment. Maddie are you OK to stay here for a while?"

"Of course. I don't think I could sit up in my flat while everything is going on. I need to tidy up here anyway and keep you all fed and watered."

"Thanks, Maddie, and don't blame yourself. If anything, it's my fault for leaving her here," I said.

"There's no point playing the blame game. What's happened has happened. We just need to find her."

Callum, Brandon, and I walked upstairs to get into Chris's flat. We had to be careful, just in case he was still in there. Knocking on the door, Callum waited to see if there was any answer. As there wasn't, he kicked in the door. Brandon stopped me from following him in.

"I think you best wait for Callum to have a look around; we don't know what we're going to find in there."

For once, I didn't argue with him. I wasn't sure I wanted to see what was in there, especially knowing that he had cameras set up in her flat. After about five minutes, Callum walked out, pulling the door shut behind him.

"Mace, I'm not sure you want to go in there."

"Callum, I need to know. I don't want to, but I need to."

"OK, but be ready. There are some things in there I'm sure you don't want us to see, so I suggest we keep it to just the three of us."

Walking into the flat, I guessed it was going to be bad, but nothing prepared me for what I was about to see.

Chapter Twenty-Three

Jessica

Coming to, I opened my eyes to blackness. Realising that I had a blindfold covering my eyes, I went to move my hand to remove it. Pain shot through my wrist as metal dug into it. What the fuck, was I handcuffed? I tried to move my other hand and was blessed with the same pain. I then tried to move my legs and found them both shackled as well.

Lying there for a second, I replayed everything that had happened this morning in my head. I was speaking to Mason and Chris came into the shop. I turned to start making him a coffee, felt a hand come round and cover my mouth, then nothing until this moment.

It couldn't be. Why would Chris do this to me? What had Sean or I done to hurt him? I had always helped him as much as I could. Hell, I even invited him into my flat for dinner as a thank you, so why was he doing this? No, I must be wrong. It must have been someone else and they got to Chris first, and now he is somewhere with Mason trying to find me.

Fear and panic started to overtake me. I felt sick to my stomach and was shaking from head to foot. Then I felt the coldness all over my body. Was I actually lying here naked? Oh God, no, please not that. Anything but that. I tried to scream, but for some reason my throat was so dry that nothing would come out.

Hearing a door open and close and footsteps coming down a set of stairs, I froze, dreading what was about to happen to me.

"Jess, babe, so pleased you are finally awake. Hope you are comfortable there. Sorry for the blindfold and cuffs, but I can't have you running away on me, now can I?"

It was Chris. I recognised his voice, but why would he do this? I tried to speak, but again my throat was too dry to make any sound, my head was pounding and fuzzy, and no matter how much I tried, I couldn't think straight.

"Sorry, side effect of the chloroform I had to use to get you here without any issues. You might feel a bit confused for a day and your throat will be dry. Let me help you with some water."

He lifted my head slightly and placed a straw into my mouth, I didn't have time to worry about what I was drinking, and I just prayed it was only water. Taking down some of the cold liquid, the relief in my throat was instant.

"Chris?" His name was more a question than a statement from my lips.

He removed the blindfold and I found myself lying on a bed, completely naked and cuffed to each bedpost. Looking around my surroundings I wished he had kept the blindfold on. What was this place, and what kind of freaky shit was Chris into? It almost looked like a dungeon down here with some pieces of equipment, for want of a better word, that I really didn't want to know how they were used.

"Yes, it's me. I'm sorry it came to this. I was hoping to bring you into my reality slowly, but Mason King put pay to that by taking you from me. Your brother had already done that to me once, so I wasn't going to allow someone to do it to me again."

"How did my brother take me from you?"

"Not you, my darling, but Nicola. She was mine. I owned her, but he put ideas of grandeur in her head and took her away from me. That's not going to happen to you. I'm going to own you until I get bored, then we will see how good you have been to decide what happens to you. But I know you will be a good girl for me, Jess."

"Chris, you can't do this to me. I have a shop to run, and I love Mason."

Then realisation struck me. I did love Mason and I hadn't told him. He may never know how much I need him and love him. I had to hope that he found me in time, even if it was the last thing I said, I would tell him I loved him. A stinging slap to the face pulled me from my thoughts.

"You will not say his name again in my presence. The only person you will love from now on is me, and you will love me, Jess. You might not think you could, but as long as you do exactly as I say, I will give you everything you need and desire. But if you disobey me, you will be punished. As you can see, I have a lot of ways to do that, and I don't think you want to try any of them out."

I lay there, just looking at him, shocked at what I was hearing. How could I love someone like this? Someone who thought chaining me to the bed was normal, and naked at that.

"Sorry I removed your clothes. I had to get some pictures. Your big brother needed to see what the consequences were of taking something from me. However, it doesn't matter, because no matter what he does, he's not getting you back. You are mine now. Even if he offered me Nicola in your place, I wouldn't want that slut back. She has spent too much time in his bed, and I don't want that.

You, however, I have time to train you to forget about the past week, for you to learn how to please me and do exactly what I want. And you will, because you're a good girl, aren't you, Jess?"

I wanted to slap him, to spit in his face and tell him I would never do what he wanted, but I had to buy myself some time. I knew they had put a camera up in the shop, so Mason would know exactly what had happened to me. I just hoped they could find me before anything bad happened. I just needed to stay calm and play along for as long as it took for them to find me.

"I'm a good girl, Chris, but you will have to give me time to process all this. I promise to be good and listen, but please don't go too fast. I just need to adjust to your lifestyle. It's all so scary and strange to me."

Where the hell that came from, I do not know, but it seemed to please Chris. So it had the desired effect. He gently brushed his hand over my cheek and placed a soft kiss on my forehead.

"Good girl, Jess. I knew you would see it my way. I will do as you ask and take things slowly. If it means you will be mine forever, then that is all I want. And I might not need to get rid of you, because if you do everything I ask, I won't get bored of you.

I'll be down in a little while with some clean clothes for you. I'll have to get some more, as I didn't have time to get any from your flat, but I have something you can wear for the moment. Unfortunately, you'll have to stay in handcuffs, but if you are good when I return, I will make you slightly more comfortable."

With that he walked back up the stairs and out from the basement.

Laying here in this dungeon, I could feel the tears starting to form in my eyes. I pushed them back as much as I could, thinking he would see this as being disrespectful to him and would end in punishment. Internally however, I was sobbing, my entire body shaking with the pain of losing Mason.

I had to keep these thoughts to myself. If he knew I was thinking of Mason, he would hurt me. I just had to hope that whatever he did, I was able to keep Mason in my mind to blank out what he was doing. I wasn't naive, I knew what he wanted from me. This dungeon explained that to me. I just had to hope that I held him off long enough to survive untouched in that way.

Still feeling quite dizzy and exhausted, I decided to allow sleep to take over my body again. Laying my head down, I closed my eyes and imagined Mason next to me, holding me and keeping me safe. Feeling the warmth and relief washing through me, I went to sleep, images of Mason in my head.

"Jess, darling."

Chris's soft voice pulled me from my slumber. Thank god I had my wits about me and didn't call out Mason's name.

"Yes, Chris," I said, trying to keep a small smile on my face.

"Since you have been good, I brought you some clothes to wear and I'm going to make you feel a bit more comfortable. I'm going to take off the handcuffs first, but remember, if you try anything you will be punished." His tone changed on the last part, telling me in no uncertain terms that he meant it.

"I won't try anything, Chris. I promise."

He paused after undoing the first handcuff, waiting to see my reaction, before undoing the second one. Helping me up, I sat there rubbing my wrists, but nothing more. I had to gain his trust, because that was my only way out of this. If he thought that I would do everything he said, then he might let me out of here and into the main house. Then I might be able to escape. It was risky, but it was the only plan I had.

Passing me a tank top, I pulled it over my head and down over my chest and body.

"I always enjoyed seeing you in these tank tops. They show all the beautiful curves of your breasts."

I internally shuddered at the thought of him watching me while I was alone in my flat, but tried not to let it show on my face. I was starting to get somewhere and didn't want to anger him.

"Sorry, but I have to put these on you. They won't hurt as bad as the other ones, but I don't think I can leave you un-cuffed, not quite yet, anyway."

He placed a pair of leather handcuffs around my wrists, but left them in front of me, so at least I could move about now and wasn't cuffed to the bed.

"Thank you. They feel much better."

He smiled, so I had obviously said the right thing.

"Jess, darling, please call me Master from now on, because that is what I will become to you in time. I will give you a while to get used to it, but if you forget too much, you will be made to remember, OK?"

What the fuck?! Who the hell does he think he is? I knew I had to play along. Lowering my eyes down, I replied. "Yes, Master. Thank you again for the clothes and making me feel more comfortable."

I felt sick saying it, but if I was going to get through this, I had to play my part in this fiasco. The smile on his face grew and I could tell I was pleasing him. I could make it, I just had to keep it up.

"For that, my darling, I will uncuff your legs and allow you to wear these shorts. You will be put back into these leg cuffs, but at least they will be far more comfortable."

Chris undid the cuffs, helped me into the shorts, and then placed the leather leg cuffs around my ankles. It was still slightly uncomfortable, but it felt 100 times better than before. Again, I thanked him.

"I have brought you some soup to eat. You will need to keep your strength up. Later I will allow you to walk around the room to make sure we don't cause any permanent damage to your legs. If you carry on behaving as well as you have so far, you could even be out of the cuffs sooner than I expected."

"Yes, Master, and thank you. I will try to do my best for you."

Every word left a vile taste in my mouth, but I knew it was for the best. The happier he was, the more he trusted me and left me alone. Chris carried me over to the table in the corner of my so-called room and placed me down on one of the chairs. He then helped me to eat the soup, while eating a bowl of his own.

About halfway through, I'd had enough and knew if I ate any more it would make me sick.

"Thank you, Master. That was lovely. However, I think I am still suffering the side effects of the chloroform and am feeling slightly sick. Could I please stop there?"

I really didn't know where this politeness was coming from. All I wanted to do was scream and shout at him, to punch him in the face with both my fists, but where would it get me? No, I was doing the right thing, even if it seemed insane.

"Jess, I'm sorry. I never wanted you to feel so sick. Let me sit you back down on the bed for a while. If you feel the need to, you can sleep. I will leave you alone until the morning when I bring you your breakfast."

Chris picked me back up and sat me on the bed, placing two pillows behind my back. Placing another gentle kiss on my forehead, he walked back over to the table and collected everything.

"Get some rest, and I'll see you later, my love."

I sat there for a while after watching Chris walk back up the stairs and out of the basement. Closing my eyes, I pictured Mason again, my safe place. And before I knew it, I had fallen asleep.

Chapter Twenty-Four

Mason

Currently I was sitting in Jess's shop, head between my legs. I had lasted five minutes in there before the need to throw up was too much, and I had to run to the bathroom. Brandon had come in a few moments later to check on me and suggested it was probably best if I waited downstairs, while he and Callum looked around.

So here I was, my brother trying to keep my mind off everything, but doing the exact opposite. Maddie had kindly made everyone coffee and was currently making us all rolls, but I really didn't think I could eat anything after what I saw.

The whole front room was full of pictures of Jess in various states of dress and undress. He had even managed to print a life size one of Jess totally naked. Then there were the cuffs, ball gags, and other items that even I wouldn't know what they were for. That was as much as I saw before I had to get out.

Slowly lifting my head to see if the dizziness had gone away, I picked up the bottle of water that Maddie had got for me after Jayden brought me down. Taking a sip, I waited for the waves of nausea to hit me again. Luckily they had passed. Sitting up, I looked around to see everyone looking at me, concerned looks on their faces. Jayden was first to break the silence.

"Mace, you OK, bro?"

"Not really, but better than I was."

"You want to talk about it?"

I would never want to tell anyone what I saw up there. Callum had been right, but I had to. I had to see what a sicko Chris Carter was. I know guys that are into that Dom shit. Not my thing, but to each their own. However, that was just fucked up to have pictures like that all over his flat. It was just a new level of weird.

"I don't think I'll ever be able to talk about that, Jayden. All I can say is he is sick, and we need to find Jess soon."

The door of the shop opened and Callum and Brandon walked through. Callum looked over to me and just gave me a chin lift of recognition. Brandon took a seat next to me.

"How are you holding up?"

"Fuck, Brandon, I don't know. I'm not sure I will ever get that image out of my head."

"I know, man. If it's any consolation, I had to walk out after a while also. We did find out how he was getting into Jess's flat, though."

"How's that?" Jayden asked.

"Through the loft space. There are no dividing walls up there so he could go from one end to the other without anyone knowing."

"Shit, I always thought I had birds or something getting in there."

"It might have been, Maddie. But chances are, if it was when he was acting weird around you, it was probably Chris."

Just then my phone went off and I saw it was a message from Jess's phone. "It's from Jess."

"Give me the phone, Mace. After what we saw up there, I'm not sure you want to open it."

Passing Brandon the phone, he opened the message, and his reaction told me immediately that I did not want to see it.

"Fuck."

Callum walked over and looked at the screen.

"Mason, I promise you we are going to find Jess. But I will say this much, if I get my hands on this guy, there might not be much left of him for you to sort out."

Jayden's phone was the next to ring.

"Sean......let me just pass you over to Callum, a detective in the Met."

"Hi, Sean, it's Callum Stevenson here...... no, under no circumstances do I advise you to open that email. Believe me, if it is the same as Mason just received, you do not want to see it. I'll send you an email address from this phone to forward it onto. We might be able to trace it, but I suspect we won't .....OK, yeah, we will see you then. I'll get one of my guys to pick you up. Send me the flight details. OK ..... no problem, speak soon.

Sean and Nicola are getting on the next flight to London. He has asked that we don't contact his dad. He would rather speak to him when we have some good news and not have to explain all this."

"So what do we do now?" Jayden asked.

"We see if we can trace the email and where Jess's phone location was when the text was sent to Mason. My guys are trying to trace the house, so hopefully we'll hear something soon. Until then, we just have to wait."

Maddie had been amazing throughout all of this and was holding up far better than me. Although she was probably just putting on a brave face and keeping herself busy so she didn't have to think about what was going on. She had made countless coffees and sandwiches for us all, as well as making sure she looked after all of Jess's regular customers like the Duncans.

Looking over at her, I could see that she was close to breaking, and tears were starting to form in her eyes. Before I could say a word, Tyler walked over to her and pulled her into a hug. For the first time that morning I was able to let a small smile form on my lips. Jess had told me that Maddie really fancied Tyler, and I had suspicions that he liked her too. Looking at them both now confirmed my thoughts.

Deciding it was best to just let them be, I turned back to Callum, who was currently looking through his phone.

"Any news?"

"My guys are currently following up a lead on a house they found about an hour away from here, just outside of Southampton. It appears to have recently been transferred to a letting agent, but we can't find any other houses linked to them. Could be a dummy business, or it could just be one starting out.

The number you were given was a burner phone and is now dead, so unfortunately that was a dead end. Whoever is helping Chris out is good, so we're going through all our usual suspects to see what they have been up to over the past few months. This has been planned, and not a spur of the moment thing. Chris was planning to do this way before Jess met you and probably before all the strange happenings in the flat started."

"I feel so useless just sitting here. Is there nothing we can do?"

"Mason, I know exactly how you feel, believe me, but you have to let us go through the process for two reasons. One, we do not want to alert Chris to what we are doing. And second, when we get him, we need to have the evidence to convict him. You do not want this guy getting off on a technicality. Jess would never feel safe again if he did."

"Sorry, Callum. Of course, I know that. I just don't know what to do. I feel as though I'm letting Jess down just sitting here."

"Mace, we all feel the same," Brandon replied. "We all feel as though we should have done more. It's easy to see the warning signs in hindsight, but at the time, you wouldn't have thought anything was strange."

It had been nine hours since Jess had been kidnapped, for want of a better word, and her coffee shop had now become an incident room. Tyler had grabbed his laptops from the office and was currently running through a number of things with Callum and a couple of his guys who had now arrived down from London.

Jayden had driven back to my place and picked up Monty, who was now sitting by my side with his head on my knee, obviously sensing the turmoil I was in. OK, it wasn't hygienic to have a dog in the shop, but I was sure under the circumstances, Jess would understand. Deciding I needed to just get out for a while, I thought I would take Monty for a walk in the park. Getting up from my seat, I put the lead on Monty and turned to the guys.

"I'm going out for some air and to take Monty for a walk. Call me if you have any news."

"You want me to come with you?"

"Thanks for the offer, Brandon, but I just need some time on my own. Don't worry, I'm not going to do anything stupid, and if I get any strange texts or messages I won't open them, OK?"

"As long as you're sure?"

"Yeah, I'm good."

Walking out the shop door, I quickly walked up the street. I didn't want to run into anyone and have to explain everything. I made it to the park without incident and let Monty off the lead. Instead of him running off into the distance as usual, he slowly walked beside me. If he wasn't a dog, I would have thought he needed this time just as much as me.

We walked together around the park until I reached my usual bench on the other side. Sitting down, I finally lost it, letting out all the pain I had been feeling since getting the call from Jayden this morning. This was what I needed, to let the hurt and anger out so I could start thinking straight. It was also the reason I hadn't wanted anyone with me, not because I didn't want them to see me cry, but because I couldn't trust myself not to throw a punch at anyone.

I wasn't sure how long I had been sitting there in silence with my head in my hands, Monty coming back to check on me every so often. Hearing a set of footsteps, I looked up to see Brandon walking towards me. He sat down next to me and didn't say a word for a while. Eventually he plucked up the courage to speak. Well, at least I guess that's what he had done. He knew how volatile I could get, and he had seen it when he gave me the news about Cassandra.

"You want to talk about it?"

"What's there to say that I haven't already said? I fucked up. I should never have left her. I shouldn't have put my business before her safety."

"Mace, we all heard the conversation you had with her. She practically begged you to go to that meeting, and she wouldn't have wanted you to lose business because of her."

"Don't you get it? It doesn't matter. If I had been here, he wouldn't have taken her. He would have seen me there and just acted as though nothing was wrong."

"You don't know that, Mace. What if he had a gun on him? He could have shot you dead and still have taken Jess. Then, even if we had saved her, she wouldn't have you at the end of it."

Feeling the anger starting to build in me again, I got up and went to walk away from Brandon before I did something I would regret, but he wouldn't leave it.

"Don't fucking walk away from me, Mace."

"Brandon, just leave it. I'm liable to do something I'll regret if you carry on."

"No, Mace, I'm not going to fucking leave it. Get your head out of your fucking arse and back in the game. Because if you don't, all this, everything we are doing, will be for nothing."

That was it, the last straw, all the anger, all the pain I was holding back, exploded with one strong fist to his face. To my surprise, Brandon just stood there looking at me. Yeah, I could tell I'd hurt him by the look on his face, but still he stood his ground, waiting for the next one.

"Let it out, Mace. Hit me as many times as you need. Just fucking let the anger out. Remember, this needs to be a mission, not a personal vendetta, because you know they never end well."

The tears started to fall as I stood there, my best friend trying to take all the hurt and anger away from me in the only way he knew how, the exact same way I would have done if he were in my shoes. I knew he was right. I couldn't allow emotion to come into this. This had to be all business. This was just another mission we had been ordered to undertake. The soldier in me immediately took over and the tears stopped. Yes, I was still worried, hurt, and angry. But I could bury those feelings until I had Jess back in my arms. It would be then, and only then, that I would let them out.

Brandon obviously recognised the change in my demeanour, now that I was in the right place, and walked over to me and placed a hand on my shoulder.

"Sorry to do that to you man, but you needed it. And if that meant pulverising my face to a pulp, I would have let you do it."

"I know you would, and thank you. Yes, I did need it, I was being a selfish bastard wallowing in my own self-pity. Let's get back to the shop. I need to see what Tyler and the guys have come up with so we can start formulating a plan."

"That's the Corporal Mason King I recognise. Come on, let's get Jess back."

Giving me a slap on the back, we started to walk back to the shop when my phone rang. It was Callum.

"Mace, you on your way back? We think we've found him."

"Be there in ten."

Chapter Twenty-Five

Chris

Nothing. I'd had absolutely no reaction from either of them. Did they not care about what I was doing to Jess? Or was it another ploy on their part? Either way I would have to play it safe.

Jess had done everything I asked of her, so she obviously did care for me and wanted to please me. I'm sure she just said she loved Mason King to anger me. If she loved him that much, there is no way she would have been so amiable to me. No, this was going to work even better than I had expected. I would have total control of the woman I now wanted in my life, and I would also get back at the bastard who had taken the love of my life from me.

I would just have to send more pictures to Sean. There was obviously no point in sending them to Mason if he didn't care. That would also work in my favour, as he didn't care what happened to Jess, he wouldn't come after me. Not that I believed what Jacob had told me. There was no way he was ex-military. He must have been confused with someone else. The Mason

King I had met was just a suit, just a nobody. OK, he had the intelligence, but no lethal instinct.

Jess looked a lot more comfortable now. I had been down to check on her and she was sleeping soundly. I hated doing what I did, but it was the only way to make her truly mine. She wouldn't have understood any other way, but she did now and she was mine.

Sitting in the living room of my Gran's old house sipping a whiskey, I thought about what the future would look like between me and Jess. She would be completely under my control, at my beck and call whenever I wanted. I didn't want kids. They were just a burden as far as I was concerned. If she did, then that was tough, and she would learn to come round to my idea. My thoughts drifted to the beautiful woman I currently held in the basement and exactly what I would do to her in my dungeon. The fun we would have, and she would enjoy it, I know it.

Jess has always come across as a shy, conservative woman, but I could see the spark in her eyes. The tell-tale signs were there that she wanted to be controlled, used, and pleasured in ways that only I could give her. Most guys didn't understand, and thought all that was required was sex to pleasure their woman. But I knew better. Control, domination, and BDSM, all combined to be the true way to pleasure a woman.

Just as I started to imagine Jess tied to my cross and me with my whip in my hand, my phone started to ring. Looking down, I saw that Jacob was calling me. What the fuck did he want?

"What?"

"Nice way to answer the phone, Chris."

"I was in the middle of something. Get to the point."

"I bet you're with that gorgeous slut in your house."

"You call her that again, and I will kill you Jacob. She doesn't concern you. I hired you for a job, so just do it and let me worry about Jess. I'll ask you again, what do you want?"

"I just thought I would let you know that I sent out the second lot of pictures like you requested, but it doesn't appear to have been delivered to Sean. I tried to track his phone, but he is no longer in the States. It would appear that he is on a flight to England."

"So I have gotten a reaction. I must admit it wasn't the reaction I had expected, but still. This is way better than I expected. Not only will I break him, but I may be able to get rid of him as well. Then I can have Nicola also."

"I thought you didn't want her."

"I don't, but I can do all the things to her that I want, all the things that I wouldn't want to do to Jess. There is a limit to the things I can do to my partner, but to a bitch like Nicola, oh, the world is my oyster."

"Has anyone ever told you, you are one sick bastard, Chris?"

"They have, but they've never said it twice. Think about that before you say it again. Find out what flight Sean and Nicola are on and follow them when they arrive."

"Sure thing, Chris. I'll let you know as soon as I have eyes on them."

Hanging up the phone without even saying goodbye, I smiled to myself. Soon I would have two beautiful women here. One I could control and care for, the other to use and abuse as I saw fit. It was every guy's dream. Well, it was my dream, and I was going to get it.

Chapter Twenty-Six

Mason

When Brandon and I got back to the shop, it was a hive of activity, bringing the soldier out in me even more. It was like being back in the ops room on a mission. This was what I needed, the perfect distraction.

"Callum, what do we have?"

"The lead on the house turned out correct. It was originally owned by Greta Carter and has only recently been transferred to South Downs Letting Agency. We looked into South Downs, and it appears to be a bogus company. It's not registered anywhere and there are no directors. How they managed to get it past all the legal red tape we have no idea, but they did. I have a couple of my men who are intelligence specialists on their way down there to check it out. They have specialist drones that won't be detected, but we'll have eyes on the place and the layout of the area. We're also keeping tabs on the phone records of Jacob Nicholls. As far as we can gather, he was best friends with Chris in Uni and a very shady character. He studied law, so that would tie in with the transfer of the property, but it also allows him to gain access to the criminal connections they would need to pull this off. I have my guys getting together a portfolio on him, so we know more."

"OK, so for the moment, we just have to wait until we get more information."

"I have gathered a SWAT team ready to go in, and they are just waiting on my orders. I know you want to be involved, but we need to do this by the book, Mace. I just need you to be there for Jess when we get to her."

"Understood, Callum. It would be a different story if we were still in the forces and on foreign ground, but I know we have no jurisdiction here. If I get to have Jess back in my arms soon, I don't care how it happens."

We spent the next two hours going through everything that Tyler and Callum's guys had found out, trying to gain an understanding of everything that was happening. Looking up at the clock on the wall I saw it was nearly 6:00 p.m., and Jess had been missing now for nearly 12 hours. I couldn't comprehend what she might be going through right now, but my only wish was she wasn't in pain.

Sean and Nicola had arrived in the UK about thirty minutes ago, and it wouldn't be too long before they arrived here at the shop. I just hoped we had more good news by the time they got here.

"Callum, Mace, the surveillance team are just sending us through the video from the drone," Tyler said, pulling me from my thoughts.

"Let's take a look," Callum replied.

"Here you go. The guys said Chris is definitely there, and they've seen him walk out of the house."

"Well, at least we know where Chris is. Jess may not be there, but

I suspect she is. I get the impression from what we saw upstairs, he wouldn't want her to be too far away."

"Is there any way we can get a layout of the house, or get a heat scan to see if we can work out where Jess is?"

"We could, but if Nicola is right and she is in the basement, we may not be able to see her heat signature. However, I will get my men on it and will see what I can do for a layout of the house."

Callum went off to call his men and I turned to Maddie. "Why don't you go and get yourself some rest? You've been here all day looking after us. You must be completely exhausted."

"What would I do? I would only be upstairs worrying my head off. You probably all need me here to keep you supplied with coffee and you need to grab some sleep yourselves. I can go upstairs and grad some pillows and blankets so you can each grab some sleep down here."

"You really don't need to do that."

"Yes, I do. I need to feel as though I am helping. I feel just as bad as you do. If I had just come downstairs with her then he may not have taken her."

"Or, he may have taken both of you. There is no point either of us beating each other up. What's happened has happened and all we can do now is focus on getting her back."

Seeing the tears start to form again, I looked over at Tyler, who was looking over at Maddie, and gave him a chin lift. He knew exactly what I was trying to say and immediately walked over to her and wrapped her in his arms.

"Come on, Madds. Let's get those blankets from upstairs so some of the guys can get some rest."

"You know, Tyler, you're the only one to call me Madds since I left home."

"I can stick to Maddie if you prefer."

"No, I like you calling me that." She finally had a smile. Taking her hand, he led her out of the shop to go and get the blankets.

"And another one bites the dust," Brandon said, as he walked over to me.

"We'll see. Jess said that Maddie really likes Tyler, and from the looks of things, the feeling is mutual. So, just two more of you to go then." I looked at Brandon and Nathan, smiling to myself.

"Yeah, in your dreams, Mace," Nathan replied.

We'll see about that, I thought to myself. Even for this small moment, thinking of something light-hearted lessened my stress a bit.

The bell on the door rang, and we all looked around to find a couple who I had to assume was Sean and Nicola.

"Sean?"

"Yes, and this is my fiancée, Nicola. You must be Mason?"

"Pleased to meet you, Sean. I'm just sorry it's under these circumstances."

"Where are we with finding Jess?"

A man after my own heart, I thought. No time for pleasantries, just cut to the chase. If I didn't know better, I would have thought he had been in the forces.

I spent the next ten minutes going through everything with Sean and Nicola. I explained exactly what had been happening and where we were with the investigation. I could see that Nicola was visibly shaken by the whole thing, even though it had been nearly seven years since she had got away from this mad man. It was clearly still bringing back a lot of unwanted memories.

"If you want to grab some rest, I can get my brother to take you to my place to get your head down for a little while."

"No, we're fine, thank you. We just want to get Jess back."

"There's nothing more I want than that, Sean. And we are working on it, but we have to make sure we do this right. We only have one shot at this and it has to be planned properly."

Maddie and Tyler had come back downstairs, and the guys from Callum's team were grabbing a quick nap in the corner. Maddie was making more coffee with Tyler, who wouldn't leave her side. I was sure he was causing more problems than actually helping, but it seemed to be distracting Maddie.

Callum walked over to us and started to speak.

"Hi, Sean. I'm Callum. We spoke on the phone earlier. I just want to reiterate that we are doing everything we can to get Jess back. Now, we think we know where she is being held, and we're working out how to get her back."
"We do appreciate it, Callum, thank you."

"Anything for Mace here. We go back a long way, and he has saved my arse more times than I care to remember. One question. Have you turned your phone back on from flight mode yet?"

"Shit, no, I haven't. I will do it now."

"No, don't. We think that it's being traced, and as soon as you turn it on, they will know you are here and probably suspect something. We've been keeping tabs on a guy called Jacob Nicholls and his communications with Chris.

I left a couple of guys at the airport, and they saw him waiting at Arrivals. We assume he found out what plane you were on and was trying to confirm if you had arrived in the country."

"Hence, why you collected us from immigration and took us out the back, so he didn't see us."

"Exactly, so at the moment we have the upper hand. From what we can gather, he sent you some more pictures of Jess, and believe me you do not want to see them. Sorry to tell you that, but they are not pretty. Nicola was right; he is a really sick bastard. His flat was full of pictures of her. Both Mason and Brandon had to leave the place. I can tell you, it is a sight that I don't think I will ever get out of my head."

I was pleased that Callum had decided to leave out the part that there were also pictures of Nicola in the flat. There were already enough people who wanted to kill Chris that were trained to do so. We didn't need Sean to add to the mix.

"What can we do to help?" Sean asked.

"Well, if you don't mind spending some time with us, Nicola, we found where Chris is currently hiding out and wondered if you could give us some insight into the house. You said you had been to his Gran's place once."

"I'll help as much as I can, but as I said, I was blindfolded when he took me there."

"Well, we know where it is now. We just need to try and work out the layout of the house. We have some plans but just need to confirm them with someone."

"OK, let's take a look."

Nicola, Sean, and Callum walked over to the laptops and started looking through everything. Standing there I could feel myself starting to lose it again, so I had to get out and get some fresh air, just anywhere other than here where I felt completely useless.

Jayden obviously sensed that I was starting to lose it again. I saw him speak to Brandon out of the corner of my eye and Brandon walk over to me. Although Jayden was my brother, he knew in times like this I needed Brandon. I loved my brother, but we clashed too much on things like this. Brandon was always the calming influence between us, and was always my go to man when I needed him or emotional support.

"Come on, Mace. Let's take Monty out for a walk. You look like you could use one also."

Attaching the lead to Monty's collar, Brandon and I left the shop and walked up towards the park again. As usual, Brandon left it a little while before speaking to me, just to gauge how to approach the issue.

"You're starting to lose that focus again, Mace. You're going back down into that black hole and you know you can't do that. Do I need to get you angry again so you punch my face? You didn't give me enough of a black eye last time."

"Hey, don't blame me for last time. That was all your fault. You pushed me over the edge."

"Yeah, it was, because you needed it, and I will do it again and again if that is what it takes to get you through this."

"You don't need to do that. I just had to get out for a while. I just feel useless at the moment. Jess has been missing for nearly thirteen hours, and there isn't a damn thing I can do about it. I just need this to be over and have her in my arms again."

"Well, now Nicola is here, and we can get a better understanding of the house and hopefully be able to launch our rescue mission."

We continued walking along in silence. The crisp autumn air was keeping most people inside at this time in the evening. During the summer the town was a hive of activity, but now with most of the holidaymakers gone, the locals preferred to be tucked in the warm. Walking around the park, the sun just disappearing from view, I noticed for the first time how peaceful it was here. It confused me that whenever I came up here it was always quiet, but today it was as if the entire universe knew that I needed peace and was giving it to me.

Taking a breath, I stopped for a moment and turned to Brandon, who had been walking by my side this whole time.

"Brandon, what if Jess doesn't want me after this? What if Chris has taken her to the point that she can never love anyone again? What would I do? I don't think I can take that kind of pain again."

"Mace, I will admit, we don't know what is happening to Jess right this moment. However, I saw how she looks at you. It would take a hell of a lot for those feelings to go."

"But what if they do? He could abuse her so much that she never wants to be touched by anyone ever again. Or worse, she might not want to live anymore. Fuck. Brandon, I don't think my heart could take that."

"Mace, I can't give you the answers to those questions, but I can promise you this. Whatever happens, we will all be there to help you. Whether we will need to help Jess cope with the situation she has been through, or whether it is to help you cope without her, we will be there."

Brandon walked over to me and placed his hand on my shoulder. Whoever said that guys shouldn't show any emotion to one another was a complete dick, because this is what I needed, to have the love and support of another guy, my best friend.

"Thanks, Brandon. I know you will all be there for me. Let's just hope I don't need it. Love you, man."

"Love you, too. Now enough of this soppy bullshit. I have a reputation to uphold, you know."

He may be the big hard man in front of everyone, but deep down I knew he was just the same as me. He often needed this kind of emotional support, especially when he lost both of his parents in a car crash a few years ago. That's why my parents often spoke to him and had adopted him as one of their own. And as soon as this was over, I would make sure all the guys went round for dinner. I just hoped that Jess would be by my side as well.

"Mace, let's get back. Hopefully they have started to formulate a plan and we can get this over and your woman back in your arms."

"Yeah, let's head back down. And Brandon, seriously, thank you."

"No need to say any more. You might be doing this for me one day."

"I hope to God I'm not, but if so, I'll be with you every step."

Chapter Twenty-Seven

Jessica

Waking up, I had no idea what the time was, and it took me a moment to realise I was still in Chris's dungeon, cuffed and unable to move. Managing to pull myself up into a seated position, I looked around my surroundings. Now I was fully awake, it was more frightening than the first time I had seen it, and I was sure I didn't want to find out what he used any of these contraptions for.

If I was clever, I could keep Chris happy enough not to use any of these on me before Mason came to rescue me. I just hoped that he was trying to rescue me and it wouldn't be too long. For a basement, it was surprisingly warm down here. I had always expected this kind of place to be cold and damp, but it was warm. I wouldn't say inviting, as it was far from that, but warm at least.

The quiet of the room allowed my thoughts to wander to Mason. Would he still want me after this? Would he forever wonder if I gave myself willingly to Chris and feel I had betrayed him the same as Cassandra? I knew for a fact that was something that

Mason would never get over, a second woman betraying him with another man. I just hoped that if I was forced to sleep with Chris, which I would do willingly to save myself, that I did it for that reason alone, to save myself so I could spend the rest of my life with Mason.

Should I give myself willingly to Chris, though? Even if it meant I was saving myself from pain and torture, was that the right thing to do? My mind was struggling to comprehend anything now, and I couldn't figure out what was the right or wrong thing to do. What the hell had Chris given me? I was so confused. The one thing I knew above all was that I loved Mason with all my heart, and nothing would take that away. I just hoped at the end of all this he would still want me.

Hearing the door to the basement open, I quickly emptied my thoughts of Mason, knowing that if I mentioned anything about him it would lead to pain and suffering for me. Footsteps down the stairs signalled the arrival of Chris again. I wondered what he would be like this time.

He was carrying a tray with two plates on it, and I had to admit that whatever it was, smelled delicious. He walked past me and placed the tray down on the table. He turned and noticed that I was awake.

"Jess, my darling, you look far better than earlier. How are you feeling now?"

"I am feeling much better. Thank you, Master. I must have needed that sleep."

I could tell he was pleased with me, as he walked over to my bed smiling at me. I shivered at the thought of him touching me, and he must have realised as his face immediately turned to concern.

"Darling, are you feeling cold? I can get you some warmer clothes if you need, or turn up the heating down here. I don't want you getting a chill."

"No, I am fine, Master. It must have been a slight breeze causing me to shiver. It is warm enough, thank you."

"As long as you're sure, my dear. I want you to be comfortable here. Speaking of comfortable, let's take off these restraints for a while. I trust you won't try anything when they are removed. I don't want to have to punish you."

"I won't try anything. You can trust me, Master."

"Good girl."

He first removed the leg restraints, obviously feeling I would do less damage that way. I sat there, but did not move, even though inside I just wanted to lash out at him. But I knew it was useless, and the consequences wouldn't be worth it. No, I had to carry on this charade for as long as I needed. The more I behaved like he wanted, the more freedom I would get, and if I was lucky he would finally allow me upstairs.

He next removed the restraints from my wrists, and again I just sat there. The only movement I allowed myself was to rub my wrists where the cuffs had been. It was nice to have them removed, however, it had not been as uncomfortable as the first time I had been restrained.

"You are such a good girl, Jess. I can see my time with you will be worth my while. It won't be long before you can join me upstairs if you continue to behave so well. I must admit I had been worried that you would disrespect me and try anything you could to escape or hurt me. It pleases me immensely that you are fully submitting to me. I hope this will continue in bed with me. The things I want to do to you, to pleasure you, I cannot wait. However, that is not for now. First we must get to know each other better and understand what we both like and enjoy. Would you please do me the honour of joining me for dinner?"

"I would love to, Master."

As if I really had the choice, I thought to myself, keeping a small smile on my face so as not to arouse suspicion. Who the hell did he think he was? This was definitely not the Chris I had gotten to know over the past five years. Yes, I thought he was creepy, but this? This was a whole new world of weird and sick.

Taking Chris's hand, I shifted myself to the end of the bed. Carefully I lifted myself to my feet and immediately felt Chris take me by the waist to steady me, stopping me from falling down onto the floor. Guiding me over to the table, he helped me to sit down. It felt good to be able to walk, even if I was still a little drowsy and unsteady on my legs.

"There you go, my dear. I hope you are feeling up to eating some food. I worry that you didn't eat much at lunchtime."

"Thank you. I'm sorry if I have made you worry, Master. I just didn't want to be ill, so thought it best to stop earlier."

"That is fine, and while we are sitting here eating, you may call me Chris. There is a time and a place for 'Master,' and the dinner table is not it."

"Thank you again, Chris. The food looks delicious."

It did look delicious, even though I really wasn't that hungry, but I knew I had to try. In front of me was chicken chasseur, and I had to admit I was impressed that Chris had made it. Taking a bite of the chicken, it melted in my mouth and I couldn't help but allow a small moan to come from my lips. Chris's chuckles pulled my eyes immediately to his.

"I will cook this more often if I get to hear you moan like that again. Although I'm sure there are other ways to get that reaction from you."

My body had a mind of its own, as it reacted to his comment with a blush to my face. Traitorous body, I thought to myself, as I looked down breaking eye contact with him. Feeling his hand close over mine and his other gently lift my head to meet his eyes, I found him smiling at me. I smiled back, knowing this would please him.

"Jess, you should never feel embarrassed around me. I love that you have this reaction to me. It shows you really care about me, and that is more than I ever dreamt of when I decided you would be mine. You are definitely more than a play thing to me. In fact, I think that I need to find someone else to play with in that way. You are far too precious to use in that way. We will have some fun down here, but I will find someone else to release my urges on. You are too pure and kind to be treated that way."

I really couldn't believe my ears. My plan was actually working. Already he was seeing me as a real human being and not some play thing he could use as he wished. I knew I wasn't out of the woods yet, but this gave me hope.

"Chris, it is OK to still call you Chris, isn't it?" He nodded for me to continue. "Thank you for seeing that in me. I know my brother has done you wrong, and I apologise for that, but thank you for seeing the real me and for caring so much for me to look after me."

I knew I was taking a gamble by mentioning my brother, but I hoped I hadn't gone too far. When I saw the smile on Chris's face, I knew I was safe. He squeezed my hand and then let go.

"Please carry on eating, Jess. I do need to look after you. And thank you for the apology, but it is not yours to make. I will find a way to make your brother pay, but it will no longer be at your expense. You are far too important to me now. I care very deeply for you. Despite how it seems, I have always cared for you, and had hoped that you would choose to be mine. So you can understand my pain and disappointment when you said that Mason King was your boyfriend."

"Chris, we both agreed never to mention his name again. Forget him. He is in the past, and if I did have any feelings for him they have long since gone. This is our time, so please do not drag up what is now in the past. And I will never mention Nicola's name in your presence."

Inside I was dying saying that to him. Of course I loved Mason, and thoughts of him were the only thing getting me through this. As long as I was still alive and untouched I knew I would be able to tell him how much I loved him. Smiling, I looked at Chris, who fortunately was smiling back at me.

"I'm sorry, darling. You're right. Those names will never be mentioned again. They are dead to both of us."

I suspected that wasn't the case for Chris, since he clearly had a vendetta against Nicola, and I hoped that would be his undoing. We continued to eat and chat about absolutely nothing in particular. If I hadn't been in the situation I was currently in, it would have been a pleasant evening.

As I sat there I could feel myself feeling drowsy again and was struggling to stay awake. It was almost as though I had taken something to help me sleep. Chris wouldn't have spiked my food, would he? I thought he was starting to trust me.

"I'm sorry, Chris. I feel extremely tired all of a sudden. Would you please help me over to the bed."

"Of course, Jess. Are you OK? You look very pale."

"I'm fine. I think I just need to get some more rest. Today has taken a lot out of me."

"Come on, let's get you into bed. I will pop down and check on you in the night, so please do not be alarmed."

Chris got up from his chair and picked me up bridal style to carry me over to the bed. Carefully he placed me down on the bed and covered me over. It hadn't escaped my notice that he hadn't put on any of the restraints.

"I think I can trust you enough to not have the restraints on now. The door upstairs is locked, so if you did decide you wanted to try and escape, you won't be able to. However, I think I know you well enough now to trust you. Goodnight, Jess my darling."

"Goodnight, Chris."

He leant down and gave me a kiss on my forehead, as I felt my eyes grow heavy, but I thought I heard one last thing before drifting off to sleep.

"I'm sorry I had to do this, Jess."

Chapter Twenty-Eight

Mason

It was nearly 1:00 a.m., and I was currently hiding in the woods surrounding Chris's hideout. Nicola had confirmed all the information we had found out about the house, and now we were here with the SWAT team ready to go in and get Jess.

Brandon was the only member of my team to come along with me, and I think Callum only allowed that to keep me from completely losing it. Jayden and the rest of the guys, along with Sean and Nicola, had gone back to my place to get some rest. However, if they were feeling half as bad as me at the moment, rest would not come easy.

We waited in the darkness of the woods for our signal to move. It was agreed that the SWAT team would go in first and disable Chris, and then we would go in after to find Jess and get her out of here. Callum was staying behind with us as well, and I think that had a lot to do with what he had seen in Chris's flat. If he got his hands on Chris, I was sure that he would kill him. At this precise moment in time, there wasn't much keeping him alive.

The lights in the house had gone out around thirty minutes ago, so the team were waiting for another few minutes, hoping that Chris would now be asleep, and they would be able to take him down without a problem.

All this depended of course on Jess being held in the basement. If she was in his bed, then that would cause more issues for the team, and another reason why I was over here and not by the house. I wanted to be there, and needed to get Jess in my arms again to make sure she was OK, but I also knew we had to do this right.

An owl hooting above us caused both Brandon and I to jump. Of all things, a bloody bird caused two grown men to jump out of their skin.

"Fuck sake, how do you get used to this, Mace? I still can't understand how you like the countryside. It's full of god knows what that could attack you at any moment in time without warning."

"You get used to it. I don't think I could live in the city anymore. It's far too loud, and look at that sky. It's great to watch the shooting stars dart across during the evening. You would never see that in London."

"Yep, Brandon, she has definitely turned him into a softy. I'll agree with you there."

I shot a look over at Callum. I may not have been his commanding officer anymore, but one look from me, and I could see the old blade coming out in him. Giving me a chin lift he recognised that this was not the time to joke around and now was the time for business. I wasn't the CO on this mission, but the respect of the old rank was still there.

I could hear Brandon quietly laughing next to me and shot him a glare too, which only caused more laughter to come from him.

He'll get it when this is all over. Placing my gaze onto the house, I could see the SWAT team getting into position. Soon this would be over, and Jess would be back in my arms. I just had to hope that she would still want to be there.

Usually it would be the case that the team would go in all guns blazing, so to speak, but Callum had hand picked this group. They were all ex Special Forces and knew the benefit of silent entry as well. I could see the lead member checking the door to see if it was locked. To his and our amazement, it wasn't. Either Chris was an idiot or he was expecting us to come.

Over the comms I could hear them questioning this.

"OK, guys, let's keep our eyes open for booby traps. This could be a setup."

Worry started to fill my thoughts., We had no idea what the guys were walking into, and this was all down to me. I was already kicking myself that I had got Jess into this mess by leaving her alone, and now I was putting a group of men in danger. I should have been used to this. I did this on a daily basis in the forces, but this was civilian life. These guys were trained in the army and navy, but they were still police officers now and not soldiers.

Callum obviously sensed my worry and placed his hand on my shoulder as he kneeled next to me.

"Mace, it's fine. They know what they're doing. That could be anyone's girlfriend in there, and they would still do the same. It doesn't matter how this happened. All that matters is we get Jess out. You're not sending anyone into their deaths, which is why I chose these guys. They're prepared for anything, and they're the best at their job."

"Callum, I know they're the best, but I'm the reason they are here. If anything should happen…"

"Forget it. If something happens, it happens. That's not on you, but on that sick bastard in there who decided to take something that didn't belong to him.

The guys have seen the pictures in his flat. I'm sorry, but they had to know what they were dealing with. Believe me, there isn't a guy there now that doesn't want to pulverise Chris to a pulp. "

"Just make sure someone keeps him away from me, because I make no promises to not touch him, even if it means me going down for him."

"There won't be any need for that. We will make sure he is out of your way and goes down for a long time."

Just then we heard the team over the radio.

"We're in. No traps so far. Think the prat forgot to lock the door. All quiet on the ground floor. We can see the door to the basement. I'm leaving two guys there and we're heading upstairs. Going Black."

That was it. We just had to wait to get the all clear. No more comms would be heard until it was all over. This was the hardest part, the waiting, not knowing what was happening. Then we heard the noise we had all dreaded, two shots rang out in the silence of the night. Callum and Brandon had to hold me back from barrelling into the house.

"Not until we have the all clear. You can't go in until then."

"We have the subject subdued. No one's injured, and the place is clear to come in."

Standing up before either of them could stop me, I was running towards the house with Brandon and Callum following me behind. I had to get to Jess, had to have her in my arms, hold her and tell her how much I loved her. Nearly taking the door of its hinges, I rushed into the house to find the SWAT team in the front room with Chris lying on the floor in handcuffs. Looking at him I could see he was a bit worse for wear. The guys had obviously been a bit free with their fists.

"So pleased you could come to my place, Mason. I'm really glad you're here. Hopefully Jess will still be conscious enough to tell you that she doesn't care for you anymore."

The more Chris spoke, the more I wanted to kill him.

"She's mine now. I own her completely, mind, body, and soul. You know she's already calling me Master. She doesn't love you, Mason, and she never did."

I felt two pairs of arms holding me back as Callum and Brandon held me back.

"Let me go! Let me at him! I will fucking kill him."

"Mace, you need to go get Jess. Leave him to us, OK?"

"Yes, I wouldn't leave it too long before you go and see Jess, Mason. She may not be with you for much longer."

"What the fuck did you do to her, you bastard?"

"Well, I had to keep her subdued somehow. I gave her some tablets crushed up in her food earlier on, but she may have had too many. There's that, along with the chloroform I used...."

Trying to break away to get hold of him, it was taking all of Brandon and Callum's strength to hold me back from fucking killing him. Before I could break free, one of the guys from the SWAT team laid him out cold with one punch.

"Forget him, Mace. Let's go find Jess," Brandon said, placing his hand on my shoulder.

We walked over to the door of the basement where the two members of the SWAT team were still standing. Opening the door Callum stopped me before I stepped on the stairs.

"Mace, we don't know what's down there. Do you want me to go first?"

"Callum, as long as my woman is down there and she's safe,

that's all that matters."

Stepping down onto the first stair I felt a hand holding me back.

"Let us go down first please, sir. We just want to check there are no booby traps down here."

Reluctantly, I let the two SWAT team members walk down the stairs first and check the area was safe. Over the comms I heard the words I was both dreading and needing to hear.

"Area clear and safe, hostage found, get a Medevac here now."

At those words, I rushed down the stairs before anyone could stop me. I looked around my surroundings for a second. Nicola was right. Jess shouldn't be here. This guy was completely sick. How could Chris think using any of this shit could be normal? And more to the point, how could he actually enjoy it?

I scanned the area looking for the SWAT guys and Jess, and then I saw her. She was lying motionless on the bed. Running over, I was by her side in seconds, pulling her up into my arms. At least she was still breathing, even if she was unconscious.

"Jess, baby, please speak to me. Please let me know you're OK."

Stirring gently in my arms, I saw her eyes open slightly, and a small smile formed on her lips. Leaning down to her, she managed to say just four words to me.

"I love you, Mason."

My heart was flooded with both joy and pain in those four words. It was almost like she had stayed alive for this long just to say those words, as though that was the last thing I was going to ever hear from her lips.

"Jess, baby, I love you too. Please stay with me. I can't live without you. Don't go. Just hold on, and we'll get you out of here in a second, but don't leave me."

I couldn't care who saw me now, while the tears were pouring down my face. She was my world, and I couldn't lose her, not now that I had her back in my arms. We had been through so much together in the past week, and I needed her with me.

"Medevac is on its way, and we found the pot of pills that Chris obviously gave her. They're only sleeping pills, but we don't know how many she's taken."

Callum spoke behind me as he placed a hand on my shoulder.

"We'll get her out of here and in hospital Mace; she's going to be fine."

"She's got to be fine. I can't live without her."

Within minutes the Medevac team arrived and were checking all of Jess's vital signs. It was serious. Her body was starting to shut down, and there was no time to spare. If Chris hadn't been taken away unconscious a little while ago, they would have been carrying him out in a body bag.

We rushed to the helicopter, and Brandon and I got in there to get to the nearest hospital. When we arrived, Jess was rushed to the emergency room, and I had to be dragged by Brandon to a waiting room. I wanted to be with her, but there was no way any of the medical staff were going to take my shit and point blankly told me to wait for news.

We had been sitting here now for over an hour. Callum and a couple of the SWAT team had arrived at the hospital for both support and to protect Jess, not that she needed protection now that arsehole Chris was behind bars. I was going to make sure that Chris fucking paid for what he had done to Jess. I would also be asking Callum to get an investigation going into Detective Jenkins to find out why the hell he didn't investigate the strange happenings in Jess's flat. If he had, we might not be here now.

Sitting there with my head in my hands, I felt so useless. The tears had stopped falling now and I was just empty. I could understand how some of the families of my team had felt when we came back from mission and they had been injured. Hearing footsteps walk into the room, I looked up to see a doctor had walked into the room.

"Are you the relatives of Jessica Davis?"

"He's her fiancé," I heard Callum say from the other side of the room.

Standing, I held out my hand and introduced myself.

"Mason King." He took it and shook my hand.

"Mr. King, I'm Dr. Jackson. Would you like to go somewhere more private?"

"There's nothing these guys can't hear."

"OK, well we've had to pump out the contents of her stomach to try and get as much of the sleeping pills out of her system. We can't see any physical damage to her body, and we also took the liberty to check if there had been any sexual abuse, given the circumstances that Detective Stevenson explained to us earlier."

That was the one thing I was dreading. What had he done to her in the past nineteen hours? Holding my breath, I waited for his reply.

"It doesn't appear that she was raped or did anything without consent."

Feeling two arms hold me, I turned to see Brandon there, just in case. Giving him a small chin lift to let him know I was fine, he let me go.

"Can I go in and see her?"

"Yes, but she is still sedated. We don't know how long it will take the drugs to wear off. She could be in a coma for a while, but we're doing everything we can. It's up to her now."

"Thank you, Doctor. Please let me know if you need anything. I don't care how much it costs."

"Thank you, Mr King. That will not be necessary. We're just doing our job. Follow me."

He led Brandon and me down the corridor and into a private room. Jess was laying there, pipes and machines surrounding her. Even though I knew she was gravely ill, she looked so peaceful, and for that I was grateful.

"I'll leave you here. If you need anything or if anything changes with Miss Davis, just hit the communication buzzer or call a nurse."

"Thank you, Doctor."

Pulling up a chair next to Jess, I sat down and took her hand in mine.

"Jess, please, if you can hear me just give me a little sign, let me know that you're OK. I need you, Jess. Please come back to me."

There was nothing, not a single movement or any kind of recognition that I was sitting next to her.

"Mace, Jess will be fine. She's in the best place now." Placing a hand on my shoulder, Brandon continued. "I'll leave you two alone for the moment and be down in the waiting room if you need me."

"Thanks, man."

I sat there in her room, the only noise being the consistent beeping of the machines monitoring Jess. Placing my head down on the bed, Jess's hand still in mine, I closed my eyes, and before I knew it I fell into a deep sleep.

Chapter Twenty-Nine

Jessica

"Jess, baby, I love you too. Please stay with me. I can't live without you. Don't go. Just hold on, and we will get you out of here in a second, but don't leave me."

The words played in my head. Had I heard them right, or was it just a dream? Did Mason really love me? Did he really mean it when he said he couldn't live without me? I could hear a persistent beeping to my left. Where the hell was I? This wasn't a sound I had heard in my prison.

Carefully opening my eyes, I struggled to see with the bright light around me. This wasn't the basement because it was far too bright and pure white. God, had I died and was currently in heaven? My eyes adjusted to the bright lights and I realised I wasn't dead, but in a hospital bed, and the beeping I could hear was the monitor I was attached to.

Looking over, I could see Jayden sitting in the corner of the room looking down at his phone. He didn't look as though he had had much sleep. Looking up, his eyes fixed onto mine.

"Hey, Jess, it's good to have you finally back. We were starting to get a bit worried for a while."

My throat was dry, and it was difficult for me to make any noise. Jayden sensed my issue, stood immediately, and held a cup of water to my lips, helping me to take some sips.

"Thank you," I managed to croak out. "How long have I been here, and where's Chris?"

"Slow down. You don't have to worry about Chris at the moment. We'll explain everything when you're feeling up to it. As for how long you've been here, it's been three days, and he hasn't left your side once. We even had to force him to eat and drink." Jayden said motioning to the other side of the bed.

Looking over, I realised that I hadn't even noticed Mason lying there with his hand holding mine. He looked terrible, even in his sleep, I smiled to myself. He hadn't left me. He did still want me after everything that had happened. I wasn't proud of what I said to Chris that I didn't love Mason and only cared about him, but it got me through both unharmed and untouched. Well, not quite unharmed, as I was currently lying in a hospital bed, but he hadn't hurt me.

Managing to remove my hand from Mason's, I carefully placed it on his cheek. Starting to stir, I watched as he slowly opened his eyes and immediately met mine. The smile that formed on his face made everything worth it, and the relief I could see filled my heart with Joy.

"Jess, you came back to me."

"Of course I came back to you. Where else would I go?"

His hand cupped mine on his face as he leaned into it. He removed it from his face and placed a gentle kiss onto my knuckles.

"I think that's my cue to leave. I'll let the nurse and the guys know you're awake."

"Thank you, Jayden, and thank everyone for getting me out of there and for looking after Mace."

"No problem."

With that, Jayden walked out of my room and closed the door.

"I thought I'd lost you. I didn't think you would ever come back to me."

"Mason, I'm here now, and I'm not going to leave anytime soon. I promised myself one thing while I was laying down there. If I ever got to see you again I would tell you that I loved you, even if it was the last words I ever said to you."

"I thought for a moment they were the last words you would say to me."

Getting up from his seat, he sat down next to me on the bed, placing his hand on my cheek.

"Jess, I have never been so scared in all my life. I have been to some of the most dangerous places in the world on missions, but nothing, and I mean nothing, compared to how I felt when I realised you were gone. My whole world suddenly came crumbling down around me and I never want to feel that way again."

Looking into his gorgeous eyes, I could see the pain and hurt was still so raw, that he truly meant everything he was saying. I just wanted to take all that pain away, to make him feel again. To be fair, although I had been scared, what had happened to me the past twenty-four hours hadn't really been that bad. Chris had treated me quite well, given the circumstances. He had taken care of me and never really hurt me physically, but I could see that Mason had suffered.

Pulling him down towards me, I placed my arms around him as

best I could with all the pipes and wires I had attached to me, and just held him. I finally knew what it was to truly love someone with all your heart, to know what it felt like to nearly lose them and then have them back in your arms. I wasn't ever going to let him get away from me. Mason gently lifted off me.

"How are you feeling?"

"Not too bad actually, just a little tired. Why am I here?"

Mason spent the next ten minutes explaining everything that had happened. They'd found how Chris had been getting into my flat through the loft. Then they'd tracked down where Chris was hiding me, with the help of Nicola. They had found Chris sitting upstairs in the house drinking. They found me unconscious, after Chris had given me sleeping pills. Laying there for a minute, I realised everything I had thought about Chris was wrong. He hadn't taken care of me. In fact, he had nearly killed me. I wondered why he made those promises to take care of me, when he was just going to kill me. I suppose we would never know, and I preferred to not dwell on it.

Mason leaned back down and took me into his arms. It was only then that I allowed the pain of the past twenty-four hours to release. Everything that I had held back for both my sanity and safety, I now allowed to flow out of me in the form of tears. Lifting slightly, Mason looked down into my eyes as the tears fell from his too. My protector, my lover, was just as vulnerable as me. It just confirmed that this was forever. The relationship we had now would be with us for eternity.

Leaning down he placed his lips onto mine, gently gliding his tongue along my lower lip, coaxing me to open my mouth and let him in. As I allowed my mouth to open, he responded by kissing me with such passion, as though it was the last kiss he would ever have. But it also didn't feel that way, because it was a kiss for new beginnings, for hope of the future. And although it was like a romantic novel cliché, it was breathtaking. I have never felt as loved and worshipped as I did just in that one kiss.

A cough behind us brought our perfect moment to an abrupt end, and Mason broke away from the kiss.

"Sorry to interrupt you love birds, but I have to check on my patient here," the nurse said as she walked over to the bed. I could feel myself blush bright red that she had caught us basically making out in my room. It was almost as bad as one of your parents walking in.

"I'll just go and speak to the guys and call your brother. He should be on his way down now with Brandon."

"My brother's here!"

"Yes, but we will chat about that in a while. Love you, babe."

"Love you too, Mace."

With that he left the room.

"Sorry to interrupt you like that, but if it's any consolation, I would have been doing exactly the same thing if I were lying there. He truly loves you, and he hasn't left your side once, even though we have all tried to get him to go and have some rest. He just wanted to be here when you woke up.

I probably shouldn't be telling you this, but he was worried you wouldn't want him anymore. He thought that you would blame him for everything that had happened, just because he left you alone to go to his meeting. It's been eating away at him for the past three days. I'm sorry, but he needed someone to talk to ,and how could I not help out a guy like him? I didn't want to cause any problems between you both."

"No, it's fine, and thank you for being there for him. Believe me, I know how easy it is to fall in love with the guy."

Smiling, she checked all of my vitals on the machine and took my blood pressure.

"You look like you're well on the way to recovery to me. I will let the doctor know, and hopefully we can get you home soon."

"Thank you."

"It's my pleasure, Jess. I'll let the guys know I'm finished and they can come see you. I must say, having you here has been a pleasure, and all the nurses will be sad to see you go, even if it is only because of all the hunks you brought with you. I don't think there is a guy in there that hasn't been given a telephone number."

"Glad to have been of service." I laughed as she left the room.

A few minutes later, the door opened and Mason walked in with Jayden and three guys I had not seen before. Looking at them, I could see what the nurse was saying, because they were all gorgeous. Not that I cared. I had my man now and was not going to give him up any time soon.

"Hey, Jess, good to see you awake. I'm Detective Stevenson from the Metropolitan Police, but you can call me Callum. I also used to be under this one's command in the Army," he said, pointing to Mason.

"This is Mark Jones and Matthew Goodhand. They were both on the SWAT team that got you out."

"Thank you, all of you, for coming to get me, and for looking after Mason."

"Anytime, Jess. It's just a relief to see you awake. We were all worried."

"Thank you for coming to check on me. If you're ever down in Kings View come in and see me and lunch will be on me. Oh God, my shop!"

Mason took my hand. "Don't worry about the shop. Maddie is looking after it along with my mother. Although I am sure Maddie would prefer not to have to deal with my mother's interfering, but when I told her what happened, she insisted she had to help."

"Yeah after she gave you a two hour lecture for not telling her sooner, I had to lie to her by saying you weren't allowed visitors just to keep her away," Jayden said.

"Well, we'll leave you now we know you are fine. I will get in touch with Mace as we'll need to chat with you at some point about what happened, but that can wait a few days."

Thanking Callum and the other guys again for everything, they left me with Jayden and Mason. After repeatedly apologising to Jayden for the trouble I had caused him with his mum, and to Mason for everything, we all agreed not to speak about it again for the day and to just be thankful it was all over.

We had been sitting for a while now, just chatting, with the odd interruption from the nurses and the Doctor who said they wanted to keep me in for one more night, just to make sure everything was fine, and then I should be able to go home tomorrow morning. Then the door opened.

Looking up, I saw Brandon walking in with Sean and Nicola. I had never been so pleased to see them both. Nicola rushed over to me, pushing Mason out of the way to give me an enormous hug.

"Jess, I'm so sorry. This is my entire fault, if I'd just....."

"That's enough. I don't want anyone else blaming themselves for what happened. This was no one's fault apart from Chris. He was a psychotic creep who couldn't take any form of rejection. This is all on him and no one else. I'm alive and no one else has been hurt, so no more, OK."

"OK, we're just glad you're OK. We were all so worried when you wouldn't wake up, and as for this worry wort here, if he could, he would have been sleeping right next to Mason."

"Hey, Sean."

"Hey, little one. How's my sis doing now?"

"I'm good. You didn't have to fly over here, though."

"Jess, of course I did. I couldn't stay at home after Mason told me what happened."

"I'll make sure you get the money back for your flights. It might take me a while, but I will give you back every penny."

"Jess, don't worry, it's all sorted. Let's just spend some time together before we have to go back home at the end of the week, OK"

We all sat there for the afternoon, chatting about how things were going for Sean and Nicola in the States and how the wedding preparations were going. Sean even formally invited Mason and the guys to come over if they wanted to.

I was starting to feel tired again, now the adrenaline had worn off with seeing everyone again, I was starting to falter. Mason noticed and suggested that everyone could meet up again at his place tomorrow afternoon, once I was settled at home. Home. It felt strange to consider Mason's cottage as home, but there was no other place I would want to be.

I wasn't going to go back to my flat anymore. There was no way I could live there knowing what could have happened if it hadn't been for Mason. After the last person left my room, leaving just Mason and me alone, he walked over and sat on the side of the bed.

"Do you want me to stay with you tonight?"

"Mace, I think you need a good night's rest more than me. You should go home and get some sleep. I will be OK here on my own. Chris is locked away, so he's not going to be coming for me. And, this is a secure wing, so no one can get in without security's say so. Just come and get me in the morning, please."

"OK, but only if you're sure. Jayden is waiting for me outside, so I can go home with him."

"I'm sure," I said as a yawn escaped my lips.

Closing my eyes, I felt Mason lean over and kiss me gently on the lips.

"Love you, Jess. Sleep well."

"Love you too, Mason."

With that, I allowed sleep to finally take me, happy in the thought that the man I loved still loved me too.

Chapter Thirty

Mason

It had been a long five days, but today I would finally have Jess back in my home and in my bed. I had never been more grateful for anything in my life. What happened between Cassandra and I was nothing compared to Jess. I hadn't gotten much sleep last night and spent most of it chatting with Brandon, who had decided to stay over as well.

It was probably best that we talked, as one of us would have had to spend the night on the couch, seeing as both Jayden and Sean and Nicola were in the spare rooms. It had been a bit of a pity party on my account, really, going through everything in my head, starting with Cassandra. It was only now that I realised, I wasn't truly in love with Cassandra. I thought I was, but it was nothing compared to what I felt for Jess.

No, Jess was definitely it for me, the last woman I would ever fall in love with, and I had a plan to make her mine forever. I had gone over it with Brandon and had asked him to fill in the guys and put everything in place. It wasn't going to happen for a while, since we both needed time to recover from what had happened, but it was going to happen, and the date and place was all set.

I had just arrived back to my house with Jess sitting next to me. I cringed when I saw that my parents were already here. I should have known that Mum wouldn't wait until this afternoon to turn up. She was going to kill me as soon as I walked through the door. My only consolation was she had probably already ripped into Jayden first.

"It's fine," Jess said next to me, as she took my hand and gave it a squeeze. "I expected your Mum and Dad to be here. I didn't think for one minute they would wait until later this afternoon."

"I know, I just hoped that we could have some time to ourselves, at least for a couple of hours anyway. Your brother and Nicola have gone down to your Dad's and are coming back tomorrow with them. So I just hoped we could cuddle up on the sofa for a couple of hours."

"I will try and get rid of them by 4:00, using the excuse that I'm tired and then it will be just us two."

"Good luck with that. Come on, let's get this over with."

I got out of the car and walked round to help Jess, to the sound of her laughter. Opening the door, she was still giggling to herself. Even though I was annoyed, it was great to hear her laugh again. Helping her out of the car, I held on to her as she steadied herself. Even though she had no physical issues from her ordeal, she was still a little fuzzy from the amount of sleeping pills Chris had given her. The doctors said this would wear off, but she needed to give it a few days.

Maddie had told her on the phone this morning not to worry about the shop, as my Mum and her were running it fine. I actually was starting to think that both Maddie and my mum were enjoying each other's company, and mum was definitely loving doing something every day and having a purpose, as she put it.

Walking up to the door, it opened before I even got there, and I moved in front of Jess just in case Monty decided to come bounding out. To my surprise, it was Dad that had opened the door, and Monty was just sitting there waiting for us to walk in.

"Hi, Jess. Good to see you safe and well my dear," my dad said as he pulled her into a hug.

"Let's get you settled in the front room with a nice cup of coffee. I would say tea, but I know you don't drink that."

"Thank you, Edward. It's good to be home at last."

Dad took her into the front room, while I went to find mum and Jayden in the kitchen. Before I could even say hello to mum, she started in on me.

"Mason Edward King, why didn't you tell us straight away what had happened to Jess? We could have come down and tried to help. And where is she now? Have you left her on her own? Do you even know what she could be going through right now and you……"

"Mum, that is enough! Give me a second to answer a question before you carry on with the next. The reason we didn't tell you from the beginning was for this exact reason. It has worried you sick and that was after we got Jess back. If you'd known from the beginning, you would have been beside yourself. Jess is currently in the front room with Dad, so no I have not left her on her own. In fact, I was hoping to have a couple of hours for just the two of us before you arrived. But as usual, you had to interfere. Lastly, yes, I do know what she is going through right now, as I have been going through the exact same thing for the past five days since she went missing and has been lying in a coma for three days. So please, can you lay off for five minutes?"

I looked over at both mum and Jayden and could see the visible shock on their faces from what I had just said. I hadn't meant to lose it in front of my mum, and shouldn't have said all that to her, but that was the only way I knew how to release the tension I was feeling. This was why Brandon would usually take me outside so I could do exactly that.

"I'm sorry, Mum. I should never have said any of that to you. I've been living on my nerves for the past five days and needed to let it all out, but it shouldn't have been at you."

Walking over to her, I pulled her into a hug. If she bit my head off now, I would have deserved everything I got. Instead, she hugged me back and then pulled away and looked right at me.

"I know you didn't mean it. Well, not in a nasty way, anyway. You did mean everything you said, and I'm sorry too. I shouldn't have jumped on you as soon as you walked in the door. We were all worried once we heard what had happened, but none of us thought about what you were going through. I haven't seen you as happy as you were when you brought Jess to see us last week. I should have realised how this would affect you."

Jayden walked over to me and slapped me on the back. "So is my soon to be sister in the front room?" I nodded at him. "Well, I best go and say hello then."

Helping mum to make coffee, we carried the mugs into the front room where I found Monty snuggled into Jess on the settee, and Dad and Jayden sat in the armchairs. Jess was laughing away at something one of them had said. Allowing mum to sit on the sofa, I sat in front of Jess on the floor, feeling her hand rest on my shoulder. We sat there for hours just chatting about everything. Jess was recalling what happened during the time she was missing. I knew she was holding back some of the information and I wondered if that was because of my parents or she just didn't want me to know.

Mum went on to the discussion of weekly shopping trips, and coffee mornings, as she wanted to spend as much time with

Jess as possible. That it was like having the daughter she never got to have. There was also a quick mention of weddings and grandchildren, much to both Jess and Jayden's amusement and my horror. I had just got Jess back, and I wanted to spend some time with her before we started to plan a wedding, but it wouldn't be long before I asked her.

After lunch, Dad convinced Mum that it was time to leave Jess to get some rest. I could have kissed him when he said it, but both Jess and I tried, not very convincingly, for them to stay, but he insisted. Jayden also decided it was time for him to get home, so it was now one in the afternoon and I finally had Jess all to myself.

We were currently cuddled up on the sofa, fire blazing, wrapped in a blanket with a film on the TV. I couldn't tell you what the film was about. I was sitting there gazing at my beautiful woman, just grateful to have her back in my arms. There were so many questions I wanted to ask her, but was too afraid of the answers. Sensing my internal struggle, Jess turned to look at me.

"What do you want to know, Mace?"

"Nothing that can't wait. I'm just gazing at my beautiful woman and realising how lucky I am to have her."

"The sooner we get it over with, the sooner we can move on with our lives. I get the feeling this is bugging you more than you are letting on."

Pausing, I tried to work out exactly what I needed to know most and how I would word it. The last thing I wanted to do was push Jess away, but there was one thing I needed to know. Before I could ask, Jess lifted her hand and cupped my cheek.

"He didn't touch me, not in the way you're thinking, anyway. He kissed me on the forehead, and that was as intimate as he got with me. Not once did he try anything sexual with me."

The relief I felt at hearing that must have been obvious as Jess smiled at me.

"I'm sorry. It wouldn't have made any difference to how I felt about you, Jess. I just needed to know so I knew how I went from here."

"I know. But I said a lot of things, things I'm not proud of and things that would probably make you extremely angry with me. But I had to say them, so I didn't get hurt."

"Whatever you said doesn't matter, unless you meant it."

"I only said one thing that I meant. I told Chris I loved you and got slapped for saying it. That was when I realised that if I was going to survive this I had to change my tactics. I'm sorry, but I can at least say this. I never once said I loved him."

Pulling Jess into my arms, I held her. We both needed this. I needed answers to my questions and she had to let it all out. If our relationship was going to work, we had to be honest with each other. It would take a while for Jess to tell me everything, but for now that was enough. Knowing he hadn't touched her or done anything to her was all I needed to know.

She looked up at me and all I wanted to do right now was kiss her and take her to my bed, but she had to be the one to initiate it. There was no way I was going to make her do anything until she was ready to do so. As we gazed into each other's eyes, it was almost as though I could see the internal struggle going through her head. She wanted the same, but was worried how I would react.

As if we both decided to test the waters at the same time, we moved our faces closer together until our lips were almost touching. I could feel her warm breath against my skin and the internal struggle of my cock that was now painfully hard trying to escape from my jeans.

I don't know which one of us made the move first, but when our lips finally touched, the electricity I felt going through my body was unlike anything I had felt before. It was more amazing than the first time I had taken her. Allowing my hands to caress her body, we were lost in the kiss, our tongues duelling in our lust filled state.

We made out on the sofa for a while, as though we were getting to know each other all over again. I loved feeling Jess's body, how responsive it was to my touch, and the moans she made as I pleasured her. She was gorgeous and even more so when the ecstasy of her orgasm took over her body.

We were now lying in bed, and Jess was wrapped around me after several sessions of love making. There was no way I would tire of this. This was what I wanted every day and night, Jess in my arms, weary from multiple orgasms. I wanted to make her mine, but knew now wasn't the time. I had to stop myself from proposing several times this afternoon, and once just as I was cumming inside her. No, I had my plan in place with the guys. it was only six months to her birthday and I would make it one that she would never forget.

Hearing her breath had slowed, I knew she was on the verge of sleep. Leaning down, I gently kissed her on the lips and whispered against them.

"I love you, Jessica Davis."

"I love you too, Mason King." She replied almost silently before I felt her completely relax in my arms and sleep took over her body.

$\mathcal{E}pilogue$

Mason

Six months had passed since everything had happened with Chris and Jess. Chris had been arrested for kidnapping and attempted murder and was currently awaiting trial. I was worried how Jess would deal with reliving everything during the trial, but I just had to remind myself that she wouldn't be doing it alone. The guys and I would all be there to support her.

Jacob had escaped capture for his role in the kidnapping and falsifying documents. As the Met already had a case on him being investigated, those charges would just be added to it. It was thought he had headed abroad and was currently residing in Turkey. Callum had spoken to the local police in Winchester who were originally contacted by Jess. It turns out that Detective Jenkins had told them all that Jess was a mental patient and shouldn't be believed. Chris had paid Jenkins off to ignore any calls from Jess, therefore paving the way to kidnapping her. I was just thankful that she came to me for help.

Since that fateful week, I was happy to say that we had been growing stronger as a couple every day. Jess had moved in with me permanently and let her flat out to a young couple who were just starting their life together, very much like us. We decided that she would keep the flat for the moment, just in case it didn't work out between us. But I didn't have to worry. Neither of us could see a future without each other.

Today was Jess's birthday, and I had already given her what she thought was her birthday gift, a new car. She wanted to be more independent and not have to rely on me getting her to and from work every day. Not that it bothered me. I loved taking her and getting to spend time with her in the shop every morning. She had been so grateful that we both ended up being late for work that morning. Luckily, Maddie had started working at the shop full time and often opened up in the morning. She was getting used to us turning up late.

That wasn't her main present, though. No, today I was going to carry out what I had been planning for the past six months. The guys had sorted everything for me and were going to get everything together this morning, ready for me to take Jess back to the cottage this afternoon. I just hoped that everything went the way I planned, or tonight could be very awkward.

Currently I was sitting in my office waiting for Jayden to arrive so we could discuss the new job we had met about yesterday. Mrs. Sienna Young had contacted us requesting help regarding her husband, although it wasn't our usual type of job. She had already employed a Private Investigator to establish her husband was cheating on her and was currently filing for divorce. However, her husband had started to make indirect threats to her because he didn't want to lose the money that came with being married to her. With the prenup he had signed, he would come out of the divorce with nothing.

That was where we came in. She had heard from a friend that we were all ex forces and had asked us to provide her with personal protection. This was something that we had all discussed when we started the company, and wasn't something that we had wanted to provide. But there was something about her request that Jayden just couldn't refuse, especially when she asked him directly to be her personal bodyguard.

Jayden walked in the door, complete with the coffee Jess had made him. It was a daily occurrence now to have coffee and croissants for breakfast and lunch delivered for those guys that were in the office. This also meant that I got to see my favourite girl during the day, as well as morning and evening. No matter what happened with the business, I was going to keep the office here in Kings View just for that one reason.

"Did Jess like her birthday present this morning? I saw it parked outside."

"Yes, she loved it and doesn't suspect anything. I can't wait for this afternoon's surprise."

"She will love it, and I am so happy for you, bro. You deserve this."

"Thanks, Jayden. Anyway let's get down to business. Sienna Young. Why on earth would you agree to be her personal protection? You know we decided not to get involved with that, and please do not tell me it's because you fancy her! She would be a client if we take the job, and that is out of bounds."

"Oh, like you and Jess?"

"That was different and you know it. We were helping her as a friend, not a client."

"Whatever you say, Mace. We all knew you liked her before you got her to stay with you. Anyway, it has nothing to do with the fact I want to sleep with her. No woman should be treated the way her husband is at the moment. The threats he is making are out of order, and someone should look out for her."

"I agree with you on that point. I'm not going to argue, but the fact of the matter is we are not a personal protection service or a security company. We are private investigators, and the fact she already has proof her husband is having an affair, she doesn't need us."

"Please, you hate dealing with cheating partners all the time. Mrs Young asked me to help her, and I want to do just that. Please don't argue with me on this. The money will be good as well."

"OK, but when you get fed up with this or dragged into the divorce proceedings as the other guy, which I suspect Mr Young will try, please do not come running to me."

He knew deep down that if that happened I would stand by him. I might say I wouldn't help, but he was my brother after all, and I wouldn't let him go down.

"I won't, and thank you. I'll set up another meeting with Mrs. Young next week to discuss the situation and how we should proceed. Is there any day you can't make? I'd like your input."

"No, any day is fine with me."

"Thanks, bro. The guys and I are going to head off in a second to set up everything for you and Jess. Maddie has snuck out to give us the picnic, so we're basically all set."

"Thanks, Jayden. I'll see you all at the cottage tonight. Tell the guys to be there for about 7:30."

"Will do. See you then."

The morning dragged, probably because I couldn't wait for it to be time to pick Jess up from the shop. Maddie was aware of part of the plan, but not the real reason I was taking Jess on a picnic. She just thought it was part of her birthday treat. No, the only people who knew the real purpose of today was the guys.

My phone buzzed and I saw it was a text message from my brother.

All set up for you

Good Luck

Getting up from my desk, I collected all my things and set out to go and get my girl. I just hoped I wasn't acting to fast this afternoon.

Walking into the shop, I could see Maddie standing behind the counter smiling at me.

"She's out back at the moment. Do you want to go through?"

"No, I'll wait here for her. Is she busy?"

"No, just making a sandwich for a customer. She should only be a minute."

Not a minute later, Jess walked out with the order in her hand. She smiled at me as she walked past to deliver the order to her customer. Walking back over, she came up to me and gave me a kiss on the cheek.

"Hi, gorgeous. What are you doing here?"

"I've come to take you away for the afternoon, and before you start arguing with me, it's already arranged. Maddie knows all about this, and my mum will be over soon to help Maddie out."

"So, I really don't get a say in this then?"

"No!" both Maddie and I said at the same time.

"OK. I'll get my stuff," Jess said with a laugh.

She walked out the back to get her stuff and moments later stood by my side.

"Keys," I said, holding my hand out to her.

"You've been dying to get your hands on that car, haven't you? Did you actually buy it for me or you?"

"Of course I bought it for you. It has nothing to do with the fact it's a Ford Mustang Shelby GT500 convertible."

OK, it did have a hell of a lot to do with that. I always wanted one, but I had my eyes on another car. For now, Jess's would have to do.

"Why am I struggling to believe you?"

"Jess, I am taking you out for the afternoon. Therefore, I should drive. Remember, it was you that insisted on driving this morning."

"Yes, and you could have stayed in bed."

Leaning over I whispered in her ear.

"Then I wouldn't have gotten to take you back to bed would I?"

Seeing her start to blush, I chuckled. I knew I had her now. She handed over the keys, and we said our goodbyes to Maddie, heading back to my office where the car was parked. Ever the gentleman, I opened the door for her and helped her down into the car. Going round to the driver's side, I got in and immediately put down the roof.

It was a beautiful spring day, and I wanted to enjoy the sunshine while it was here. Starting the drive back to the cottage, I could already see the confusion on Jess's face.

"I thought you said you were taking me out for the afternoon?"

"I am, in a way. We have to go back to the cottage first and then go for a little walk. All your questions will be answered soon enough, so you can stop sulking over there."

"I'm not sulking."

"I'm not going to argue with you today. This afternoon is going to be very special, so please just bear with me," I said as I pulled up outside the cottage.

Seeing all of the guys had already left, I breathed a sigh of relief, because that would have taken even more explaining. I walked round and helped Jess out of the car and guided her towards the back of the cottage. As we went around the corner Jess gasped in amazement.

It was perfect. The guys had done a great job and even better than I had imagined. They had draped the pergola with material and fairy lights, laid a picnic blanket on the ground, and placed all the food out onto it. There was a big bouquet of flowers, a bottle of wine, juice, and two glasses.

"It's beautiful. Did you do this all by yourself?"

"I'm not going to lie, the guys did all the hard work. Maddie got the picnic together for me, but it was my idea, if that makes you feel better."

"Thank you," she said as she gave me a kiss.

"Come on, let's enjoy the food Maddie has prepared for us."

I had no idea what to expect, but it looked amazing. Sandwiches, savoury pastries, cakes, chocolates, and strawberries. The girl had done well.

Helping Jess down, we both sat on the cushions that the guys had obviously thought we would need for comfort, and started to eat the picnic while we sat and chatted about our day.

"Wine?"

"No, thank you. I will leave the wine for the moment and just have a glass of juice, thank you."

"Worried I'll take advantage of you in a tipsy state?"

"You would take advantage of me no matter what state I was in," she said laughing away.

"You know that's not true. I would never take advantage of you if you weren't completely in control of yourself."

"I know, I'm only joking."

We sat there enjoying the warm spring afternoon, enjoying each other's company. We needed to do this more often. Turning to me, Jess said, "That was delicious, but I couldn't eat anything else. We really should do this more often."

"I was just thinking the same thing. Perhaps we should make this a monthly occurrence? However, I don't think I can convince the guys to do this every time. This was a special occasion."

I packed what was left of the picnic back into the basket, put it to one side, and pulled Jess into my lap.

"You did this all for my birthday?"

"Well, yes and no. I still have one more present that I want to give you, and I needed a special way to do it."

"Another present? Mace, the car out there must have cost you a fortune. You really didn't need to give me anything else."

"I did need to get you one more thing. It's not really a birthday present, but I couldn't think of a better way to give it to you. However, to get it, you need to stand up."

"Stand up?"

"Just humour me for a second, will you please?"

"OK."

I helped her up from the blanket and stood in front of her, holding both her hands in mine. Placing a gentle kiss on her lips, I let go of one of her hands and got the box out from my pocket. Getting down onto one knee, Jess put both her hands on her mouth as she gasped. Opening the box, I took her hand in mine.

"Jess, I fell for you the very first time I spoke to you, and after nearly losing you forever, I want to make sure that we are together forever. So, Jessica Davis, will you do me the honour of becoming my wife?"

I waited, still kneeling on the floor as I looked up into her now tear-filled eyes. This was the worrying moment. Would she say yes? I was really starting to worry the longer she didn't say anything.

"Jess?"

"Mason King, could you have made this day any more perfect?"

"Is that a yes?"

"I couldn't think of anything I would rather have. Yes, of course I will marry you."

Placing the ring on her finger, I got up from my knee and grabbed her in my arms, lifting her from the ground and spinning her around. Putting her back down on her feet, I pulled her to me and kissed her, pouring as much love and feeling as I could into it.

"Mum is going to be so pleased when I tell her. The only problem will be that she'll want to take over the planning of the wedding. I hope you're ready for that?"

"As ready as I'll ever be. As long as I get to choose the dress and you will be there, I don't care about anything else."

Sitting back down on the blanket, I pulled her back into my lap and held her close. We sat there in each other's arms for a while.

"I thought we might get married in October, maybe on the date when we first got together."

"That would be nice, but there is one thing, though. You might want to put off the wedding for a while longer, say this time next year."

Shocked at her statement I took her hand in mine.

"I thought you would be happy. Why would you want to put it

off?"

"Well, that would be because brides are meant to look absolutely fabulous on their wedding day, not fat and unattractive."

"Jess, you are absolutely gorgeous, and you are definitely not fat and unattractive."

"But I will be."

Confused by what she said, I just sat there holding her hand, gazing at her. She obviously understood my confusion because she leaned towards me and placed a soft kiss on my lips and then whispered in my ear.

"I'm pregnant."

About the Author

Clarice Jayne is a new Author who published her first book Jessica's King in April 2021.

Living in Kent, The Garden of England, with her husband, daughter and dog, she started writing as a hobby when someone suggested she should publish a book. Jessica's King was the outcome.

Clarice writes mystery romances based in the south of England. All of her books include mystery, a little danger, passion, family, and a happily ever-after.

When she is not writing, Clarice works full time in the healthcare industry, drinks copious amounts of coffee and enjoys spending time with her family.

Next from Clarice Jayne
Sienna's King

Jayden King followed in his brother's footsteps and joined the army, but that is where the similarities end.

Whereas his brother, Mason, wanted to be happily married with 2.4 children, Jayden is happy to play the field and enjoy his bachelor lifestyle. That is until fate, and his current assignment, brings Sienna Young into his life

Sienna Young is a member of the country's elite. Born to privileged parents, she has always had the fine things in life. Married to a man she thought was the love of her life, she now finds he has been cheating on her, since their wedding day.

Seeking the help of King Brothers Investigations, after physical abuse and threats from her husband, Jayden and Sienna are thrown together for her safety. However, it soon becomes apparent that more is at stake, when someone from the King brother's past plays a significant role in the situation.

When does protection become more than just a job for Jayden, and can that protection come in time to save the woman, he has grown to love?

Sienna's King is a stand alone mystery romance with a happy ever after, and is the second book in the King Brothers Investigation series.

Also from Clarice Jayne

Kings Brothers Investigation Series

Jessica's King

Sienna's King – Coming Summer 2021

Printed by Amazon Italia Logistica S.r.l.
Torrazza Piemonte (TO), Italy

39857590R00147